Merry Christmas to Willie (Willy, Will, or is it Bill or Bi
well anyways YOU know who I mean.
This book is For you, I hope you
like it. It's a book of

TALES THE WIND TOLD   me.

Love your sis
   Annie, (I'm the
      one you
      call Sharon.)
      hee hee.

MARIE MRŠTÍKOVÁ

Tales the Wind Told

ILLUSTRATED
BY LUDĚK MAŇÁSEK

HAMLYN
LONDON • NEW YORK • SYDNEY • TORONTO

TRANSLATED BY PAUL WILSON
Designed and produced by Artia
Published 1974 by the Hamlyn Publishing Group Limited
London ● New York ● Sydney ● Toronto
Astronaut House, Feltham, Middlesex, England
This edition © 1974 by Artia, Prague
Printed in Czechoslovakia by Svoboda, Prague
ISBN 0 600 387046
1/01/23/51

CONTENTS

IT DOESN'T HAPPEN TO JUST ANYONE, but as Willie can tell you, it really did happen to him.

It was a dark, bitter cold winter evening, and the wind was singing in the chimney. Willy should have been in bed and asleep long ago, as his Granny had ordered, but he wasn't. He was sitting by the fireplace watching the burning logs. That was what he liked best of all about being at Granny's, the logs burning on the hearth. Neither he nor any of his friends in the city had fireplace: Granny was the only one he knew who had. Whenever Willie came to visit her in her old cottage in the woods, she always lit a fire for him at least once every few days. But this time the fire had been going for almost a week, for Willie was ill and he needed the warmth. That was why he should have been in bed sleeping.

But Willie sat and looked into the flames until he began to see spots dancing before his eyes. Sparks jumped from the burning logs, changed into fiery little men, and these little men danced and whirled about before flying up the chimney. And above the chimney, above the roof, even above the tree tops, they became transformed into stars.

The dancing sparks made Willie's head spin. It was time to go to bed, he said to himself, but as soon as he said this the wind in the chimney began to sing even louder than before, and something jumped out of the fireplace. It wasn't a spark, and it wasn't a fiery little man; Willie would have chased him away if it had been. No, it was something quite different. It was a tiny little girl with golden hair and eyes like deep green pools of water.

"Who are you?" said Willie in astonishment.

"Curiosity killed the cat," laughed the little girl. "Don't ask questions, and let's play instead."

And she gave Willie a light tap and said, "Let's play tag." So they played tag for a while, and then hide-and-seek, and then hide the slipper, and when they had had enough, they sat down in front of the fire again. Then the little girl made tiny figures — animals, trees, and people — from the ashes, and whatever she made immediately came to life and moved and ran about until she blew on it. Then it became a handful of ashes once more.

Willie could hardly believe his eyes. He'd never seen a game like this before, but the little girl knew it already and very quickly tired of it, so she said, "Tell me a story."

9

"But I don't know what to tell you," said Willie, who was taken aback by her sudden request.

The little girl had just made four little figures from the ashes, three boys and a little girl. "Tell me a story about these three little boys and that little girl," she said.

Willie hardly knew what to say. "I could never do it myself," he said, "but if you like we can look through these old books. Granny always reads me stories from them. Perhaps we can find something there."

And so Willie and the little girl looked through the books until they found the fairy-tale they were looking for. They brought the book over to the fire, lay down in front of it, and Willie began to read very slowly and clearly. And this is what he read.

JOHN, JOSEPH,
STEPHEN, AND BEAUTIFUL SIMONE

Once upon a time there was a woodcarver who made wooden shoes and sold them at the fair. But do you think a woodcarver can make a living when all his neighbours are as poor as he and haven't enough money even for a pair of wooden shoes? So the poor woodcarver could hardly make both ends meet, and the more children he had, the worse it became. It wasn't long before there was an even dozen, all boys, and his little cottage in the middle of the woods was full to bursting. And then a thirteenth was born — a very pretty little girl.

No sooner had she been born than the poor woodcarver set out from his cottage in the woods to find a godfather for his daughter. At the very edge of the woods, as luck would have it, he met the gentleman to whom the woods and everything around it belonged.

"Good day, woodcarver!" said the gentleman. "Where are you off to in such a hurry?"

"Good day to you, sir," replied the woodcarver. "I'm off to the village to look for a godfather. I have twelve sons, and now I've just had a daughter as well."

"Well if that is the case, I'll be a godfather to your daughter," said the gentleman. "And not only that. If you wish, I shall take her to live with me in the manor house and I shall raise her as if she were my own."

The woodcarver did not like the idea of giving up his only daughter, but at least, he thought, she would have an easier life than he and his sons. So he nodded in agreement.

And so the gentleman took the little girl and raised her in the manor-house as if she were his own daughter. He had three sons, John, Joseph and Stephen, and now they had a baby sister. They called her Simone.

The boys loved little Simone with all their heart. When she was still very small, they played with her all the time and when she began to grow up, they went horse-back

11

riding with her and took her hunting with them. They grew up together as one happy family, for they did not know then that she wasn't their real sister.

They learned the truth when they were almost old enough to get married. One day they wanted to go riding somewhere, and they ordered the servant to saddle the horses for them.

"Be quick about it," they commanded, somewhat rudely, "and saddle one for Simone as well."

The servant was annoyed at their manners and snapped, "I'll saddle the horses for you because you are the sons of my master, but I'll not saddle a horse for that woodcarver's daughter."

"How dare you say such a thing!" the boys shouted.

"It's the truth!" replied the servant. "Just ask your father!"

The boys ran to their father and Stephen, the youngest, asked, "Father, is it true that Simone isn't our real sister?"

"Yes, it's true" answered the gentleman. And then he told his sons how it had all happened. At first the boys could scarcely believe their ears, but soon their astonishment turned to joy. And the happiest of all was young Stephen.

"If Simone isn't my sister, so much the better, for I can take her as my wife!" he exclaimed.

But the gentleman stopped him. "Wait, Stephen," he said. "You are forgetting that you're the youngest."

"That's right," said the oldest son, John. "I shall marry Simone."

"And what about me?" put in Joseph.

"Enough bickering!" said the gentleman. "Simone shall marry the one who most deserves it. Here is a thousand ducats for each of you. Go into the world, and the one who brings back the best gift may have Simone as his wife."

And so the brothers set out into the world. And because they were truly good brothers, they went together. They rode and rode until at last they came to the city of Paris. And there they went their separate ways to buy gifts for their beloved Simone.

The oldest brother John was the first to buy his gift. In a certain street he saw a crowd of people around a shop, looking at coaches, and each coach was more beautiful than the next.

"I'll buy Simone a coach like that," John decided. "But it must be the best and the most expensive one."

And he went to the coachmaker and asked him to show him the most expensive coach he had.

"My most expensive coach is this one here," said the coachmaker, pointing to an ordinary-looking wagon standing in the corner of the yard. "It costs an even thousand ducats."

John was astonished. "And what's so special about it, that it should cost a thousand ducats?" he asked.

"This coach is the only one of its kind in the world," said the coachmaker. "All you have to do is sit in it, and in the wink of an eye, it will take you wherever you wish, even without horses to draw it."

"That is truly a rare coach," said John happily. "Neither of my brothers will have a gift like that." And he gave the coachmaker his thousand ducats.

While John was buying this magic coach, Joseph stopped at a jeweller's shop.

"I shall buy Simone a beautiful piece of jewellery," he said, and he asked the jeweller to show him his most expensive item.

"The most expensive item I have is this," said the jeweller, and showed Joseph an ordinary pair of glasses in wire frames. "They cost an even thousand ducats."

Joseph was astonished. "And what's so special about them, that they should cost a thousand ducats?" he asked.

"This is the only pair of glasses of its kind in the world," said the jeweller. "All you have to do is put them on, and you will be able to see anything you wish even if it is a thousand miles away."

"These are rare glasses indeed," said Joseph happily. "Neither of my brothers will have a gift like that." And he gave the jeweller his thousand ducats.

While Joseph was buying his magic glasses, the youngest brother Stephen stopped by a green-grocer's barrow. He was terribly thirsty and he had caught sight of three beautiful apples smiling at him from the old lady's basket.

"How much are those apples, old woman?" asked Stephen.

"An even thousand ducats, young man," replied the old lady.

Stephen could scarcely believe his ears. "And what's so special about those apples, that they should cost a thousand ducats?" he asked.

"They are the only apples of their kind in the world," said the old lady. "All you have to do is eat them and you will get well, even though you be on the very edge of death."

"They are rare apples indeed," said Stephen happily. "Neither of my brothers will have a gift like that." And he gave the old woman his thousand ducats.

He wrapped the apples in his scarf and hurried off to meet his brothers. John came up in his coach, and Joseph was carrying his glasses.

"Well, have you bought what you wanted?" asked the oldest brother John.

"We have," answered the others.

"Then let's go for a ride around Paris and afterwards we shall set out for home," said John, inviting his brothers to step inside the coach so that he could show off his gift.

"But first let's see how things are at home," said Joseph, because he too wanted to show off. But as soon as he set the glasses on his nose he cried, "Quick, on your horses, brothers! Father and Mother are on their death bed, and our beloved Simone too!"

"Let the horses be, and jump up here with me," said John. "My coach will take us there in the wink of an eye."

And sure enough, no sooner had they sat in John's coach and blinked once, than they were home. And none too soon, for had they come any later, they wouldn't have found their loved ones alive.

The brothers stood in tears by the sickbed, but Stephen did not cry. He gave his father, his mother, and dear Simone each a magic apple and said, "Eat them. They will help you."

And the apples did help. After the first bite, they began to feel better, and by the time they had eaten them all up, they got out of bed and joyously hugged and kissed the three brothers. But when the time came to decide which brother, John, Joseph or Stephen, should have Simone for his wife, the quarrelling began.

"Without my glasses, you wouldn't even have known they were ill," said Joseph, who felt he should be the one to have her.

"Without my coach we wouldn't have come in time," insisted John.

"And without my apples, they wouldn't be alive and well at all," said Stephen.

"Enough bickering!" said the gentleman. "I shall be the judge. It is true that without Joseph's glasses, you wouldn't have known of our illness. And it is also true that without John's coach you wouldn't have come in time. But without Stephen's apples, we would this day be lying in our graves, and so would Simone. And besides, you still have your rare gifts, the glasses and the coach. But Stephen sacrificed everything for us, and now he has nothing. All the more reason why he deserves the beloved Simone."

John and Joseph saw that their father was right. But the happiest of all was Simone, for after all, it was Stephen she loved the most. And so everyone was content. In a week Stephen and Simone were married, and it wasn't long before John and Joseph found wives and were married too, and so they all lived together happily ever after.

WHEN WILLIE FINISHED READING, ALL WAS QUIET except for the fire crackling in the fireplace and the wind singing in the chimney. "Read me another one," the little girl said.

But Willie was somewhat sleepy by now. "It's your turn," he yawned.

"I can't read," laughed the little girl.

"Then tell me one you know," said Willie.

"I don't know any either," she laughed again. "But if you want, my Mother will tell you a story. Listen!"

And she put her finger to her lips. By now Willie could hardly keep his eyes open, but in spite of this, he heard a musical voice in the chimney, almost as if someone were singing a lullaby, and then, in a still, quiet voice, the Wind began to speak. And this is the story she told.

THE PRINCE
AND THE SILVER RABBIT

Once upon a time there lived a rich and powerful King who had everything he could wish for. He had a wife and four children, a son and three fair daughters, but even so, he was not happy. And how could he be, when the court astrologer, who could read the future in the stars, had told him that his dear daughters were in grave danger? Before they reached seventeen, the astrologer said, they would disappear and the King would never, ever see them again.

Naturally the King was very upset by this prediction, and day and night he tried to think of ways to keep his daughters from harm. Finally he decided to have a very high wall built round the royal castle and its gardens, and to place a strong guard around it. Behind the wall, under the protection of the guards, the Princesses would be safe.

While the dear Princesses were not allowed to go a single step beyond the castle and its gardens, their brother went into the woods every day to hunt. He loved hunting, and when he was chasing after game, when he heard the baying of the hounds and the trumping of the horns, he was the happiest young man in the world. But his happiness did not last long. One day, when the good Prince returned home from the hunt, he was greeted by great weeping and lamentation. His oldest sister had disappeared from the garden like a leaf carried off by the wind, and no one knew where.

The old King's heart almost broke with sorrow and the Queen was so grief-stricken that she took to her bed. The good Prince no longer enjoyed hunting, for nothing could take his mind off his lost sister. He had a double guard placed around the castle and the garden, and he forbade his two sisters to go any further than the courtyard. But even that did not help. Scarcely two weeks had gone by when once more he returned home only to be greeted by great weeping and lamentation. His second sister had suddenly disappeared from the courtyard like a blossom blown away by the wind, and again no one knew where she had gone.

16

It was a terrible blow for the old King and as for the poor Queen, she almost died of grief. They placed their last remaining daughter under a triple guard and forbade her to go outside, even into the courtyard. But all in vain. Scarcely a week had gone by before the good Prince returned to the castle one evening to be greeted a third time by great weeping and lamentation. Whilst he was hunting, the third princess had disappeared from the castle itself and was gone like a rose-petal blown away by the wind. But where she had gone, no one knew.

The old King and the Queen could no longer bear the great burden of grief, and they soon died. The good Prince remained alone in the royal castle and for a long, long time he mourned his parents and his lost sisters. He never set foot outside the castle, never went into his beloved woods to hunt. But at last, when time had lessened his grief, he went out once more, all alone. And a very strange thing happened to him. Suddenly, in a meadow, he saw before him a rabbit with silver fur, and the rabbit was sitting and looking at him fearlessly with exquisitely beautiful eyes.

The moment the Prince caught sight of the rabbit, he forgot his sorrow at once and could think of nothing else except how to catch it. He went up to it slowly, reaching out his hand, and just when he was about to take hold of it, the silver rabbit hopped away and was gone. But it didn't leave the meadow. It sat down again in the grass some distance away and once again looked at the Prince with its exquisitely beautiful eyes, as if it were inviting him to come nearer. The Prince did not hesitate for long, but once more went up to it slowly, holding out his hand, and once more the rabbit hopped away just as he was about to catch hold of it.

And so it went the whole day. All day the good Prince chased the silver rabbit, and all day the rabbit hopped away from him, without really running away. When darkness began to fall over the wood, the Prince was far, far away from his castle and the forest stretched away on all sides, without a single house in sight. The good Prince was exhausted, and stopped under a spreading oak-tree.

"I have been chasing this rabbit all day and now, just because of it, I shall have to sleep under the stars!" he sighed.

And he made ready to lie down under the oak-tree. But before he could stretch out, the silver rabbit spoke to him in a human voice.

"Why should you sleep under the stars, when a bed is awaiting you close by," it said.

The Prince was astonished. "A bed?" he said. "And where might that be?"

"If you don't wish to sleep under the stars," said the silver rabbit, "then follow this lane of oak-trees until you come to a castle. There you will be welcomed with open arms, believe me."

And with that, the silver rabbit disappeared, as if the earth had swallowed it up. Without hesitating the good Prince followed the lane of oak-trees, and sure enough, it wasn't long before he was standing in front of an old castle surrounded by a high wall. He pounded on the gate with the hilt of his sword.

"Open up, good people, open up! Let in a hunter who has lost his way," he cried.

Almost before he knew it, the castle gates swung open, and on the threshold stood the Prince's oldest sister. She had recognized his voice and run to open the gate herself.

"Welcome, my dear brother," she cried. "You don't know how glad I am to see you in this wilderness!"

Then she lovingly embraced the Prince and led him into the castle. She had the table spread with delicious food, and while the hungry Prince was eating and drinking, she told him all that had happened to her. She had been carried off from the garden by a powerful giant who was the lord of this castle and master of all the antlered animals in the forest.

"Now I am his wife and I love him, even though I am a little sad here all alone. I would be overjoyed if you could stay here and pass the time with me, but I'm afraid for your safety. My husband went out hunting this morning, and when he returns, he could very well eat you, especially if he doesn't bring back enough. He has a ferocious appetite, and for supper he eats half-a-dozen oxen at one sitting."

The Prince was frightened at first, but then he said.

"Perhaps it won't be as bad as you think, sister. Since I'm here, I'd like to meet your husband too. Hide me somewhere, so that I can have a look at him first, and then in the morning I'll go on my way."

So the oldest sister hid the Prince behind a row of casks at the other end of the hall. No sooner had she done this when the door flew open with a terrible clatter and the giant strode into the room. He threw half-a-dozen dead oxen on the table and said, "Here is my supper."

And then he took off his cape, which weighed a good five hundred-weight, threw it over the casks, and sat down to the table.

"I'm tired, woman. Get me something to drink," he said.

The oldest Princess took a bucket, filled it with wine from one of the casks and set it in front of her husband. Grasping the bucket in both hands, the giant lifted it to his mouth, but as soon as he sniffed the wine, he began to shout, "Woman, this wine smells of man. Speak up! Who are you hiding here? Where is he? I want to see him, or there will be trouble!"

"Don't be so angry, my husband," said the oldest Princess, trembling. "It is only my brother, who has come to visit me for a while. Do not harm him, I beg of you."

The giant calmed down. "If it is your brother," he said, "then no harm shall come to him. He shall dine with us, for there is food enough. But where is he? Show him to me, that I may see him!"

The oldest Princess went over to the casks, took her brother by the hand, and led him to the giant.

The giant took an instant liking to him.

"Your brother is a fine fellow, wife!" he roared. "Never fear. I shall not harm him. Why, I know him already. I saw him only today in our woods!"

Then he turned to the Prince. "Sit down, brother-in-law. Drink with me and while your sister is preparing supper, tell me how long you've been chasing after that silver rabbit."

"All day," replied the Prince. "And tomorrow I shall go after it again until I catch it!"

The giant roared with laughter. "My dear fellow," he said, "so you intend to catch the silver rabbit. Remember this: I have been after it these five years and to this day I haven't the slightest idea where it hides when I lose sight of it."

But the Prince would not be put off. "Be that as it may," he said, "I shall continue the chase, and we shall see."

The giant shook his head. "Believe me, brother-in-law, you would do better to stay here in peace with your sister, and forget about the silver rabbit."

But the Prince shook his head. "No, brother-in-law," he insisted, "I'm going to try again. Perhaps I shall have better luck this time."

"Very well," said the giant, "if that is what you wish, then I shall help you as much as I can. Here is an ivory horn. If you need something, just blow on it, and I'll come to your assistance."

The Prince took the horn, thanked the giant, and went to bed. Early next day, they both set out. The giant, as usual, went hunting in his woods, and the Prince went searching for his silver rabbit. He found it as soon as he came to the first meadow, and he chased it the whole day long. Each time he thought he had caught it at last, the rabbit would hop out of reach at the last moment and then sit in the grass a little further on. Towards evening, when it began to get dark, the Prince sank exhausted to the ground under a chestnut tree and sighed, "I've been chasing this rabbit the whole day and now I must spend tonight under the stars once more because of it."

But before he could stretch out, the silver rabbit spoke to him again in a human voice.

"Why should you sleep under the stars when a bed is awaiting you close by," it said.

The Prince was astonished. "A bed? And where might that be?"

"If you don't wish to sleep under the stars," the silver rabbit replied, "then follow this lane of chestnut trees until you come to a castle. There you will be welcomed with open arms, believe me."

As soon as it had said this, the silver rabbit disappeared as though the earth had swallowed it up. Without another thought the good Prince followed the lane of chestnut trees, and very soon he was standing before an old castle with a high wall around it. He pounded on the gate with the hilt of his sword and cried out, "Open up, good people, and let in a poor hunter who has gone astray."

And it wasn't long before the castle gates swung open and there on the threshold stood the Prince's second sister. She had recognized his voice and run to open the gates herself.

"Greetings, my dear brother. You have no idea how happy I am to see you in this lonely place!" she cried.

And she immediately embraced the Prince lovingly and led him into the castle. She spread the table with good food and while the Prince was eating and drinking, she told him what had happened to her. She had been carried off from the courtyard of the royal castle by a powerful giant who was the lord of this castle and master of all the birds of the air.

"Now I am his wife, and I'm happy with him, though I sometimes miss being among people. I would be overjoyed if you could stay here and keep me company, but I fear for your safety. My husband went hunting in the morning, and when he returns this evening, he could very well eat you, especially if he didn't catch enough for supper. He eats a dozen oxen at one sitting."

But the Prince would not be dissuaded. "Perhaps it won't be as bad, as you think, sister," he said. "Since I'm here, I'd like to meet your husband anyway. Hide me somewhere here so that I can have a look at him first, and then in the morning, I'll go on my way again."

The second sister hid the Prince behind a row of barrels at the other end of the hall. No sooner had she done this when the door flew open and the giant stepped into the room. He threw a dozen dead oxen on the table and said, "Here is my supper."

And then he took off his cape, which weighed a good seven hundred-weight, threw it over the barrels, and sat down at the table.

"I'm tired, woman. Get me something to drink."

The second Princess took a tub, filled it with wine from the barrels, and set it in front of her husband. The giant fell upon the tub with both hands, raised it to his lips, but when he had sniffed the wine, he set up a great commotion. "Woman, this wine stinks of man. Speak up! Who are you hiding here? Where is he? I want to see him, or there will be trouble!"

"Don't be so angry, my dear," said the second Princess uneasily. "It's only my brother, who has come to see me. Do not harm him, I beg of you."

The giant calmed down. "If it is your brother," he said, "then no harm shall come to him. Let him dine with us, for we have food enough. But where is he? Show him to me!"

The second Princess went over to the barrels, took her brother by the hand and led him to the giant.

The giant liked the Prince immediately.

"Your brother is a fine fellow, wife!" he said. "Never fear. I won't lay a finger on him. Why, I know him already! I saw him only today in our woods!"

And then he turned to the Prince. "Sit down, brother-in-law. Drink with me and tell me how long you've been chasing that silver rabbit."

"For two whole days," replied the Prince. "And tomorrow I shall go after it again until I catch it!"

The giant roared with laughter. "My dear fellow," he said, "so you intend to catch the silver rabbit! Remember me well: I have been after it for seven years now and to this day I haven't the slightest idea where it hides when I lose sight of it. You would do better to stay here in peace with your sister and forget about the silver rabbit."

"No, brother-in-law," insisted the Prince, "I shall give it another try."

"Very well," the giant said, "if that is what you wish, then I shall help you as much as I can. Here is a bird's beak. If you need something, whistle on it, and I shall come to your assistance."

The Prince took the beak, thanked the giant, and went to bed. Early next day, they both set off, the giant as usual to hunt in his woods, and the good Prince to seek out the silver rabbit. He found it as soon as he stepped into the woods, and he chased it in vain, the whole day long, as before. When evening came, the exhausted Prince sat down under a spreading beech-tree and sighed, "I've been chasing this rabbit all day long, and now I must sleep beneath the stars all night."

But before he could stretch out in the grass, the silver rabbit spoke to him for the third time in the language of humans. It said, "Why should you sleep under the stars when a bed is awaiting you close by."

The Prince was astonished. "A bed? And where might that be?"

"If you don't wish to sleep under the trees," the silver rabbit replied, "then follow this lane of beech trees until you come to a castle. There you will be welcomed with open arms, believe me."

And as soon as it had said this, it disappeared like a stone dropped into the water. Without delay, the good Prince followed the lane of old beeches and in no time at all he saw before him an old castle with a high wall on every side. He pounded on the gate with the hilt of his sword and cried out, "Open up, good people, open up, and let in a poor hunter who has nowhere to go."

And it wasn't long before the castle gates opened and who should be standing on the threshold but the Prince's youngest sister. She had recognized who it was by the voice and ran to open the gates for him.

"Please do come in, my dear brother," she said. "You have no idea how overjoyed I am to see you in this secluded place."

And she embraced the Prince lovingly, led him into the castle, and gave him a meal fit for a king. While the hungry Prince was enjoying his supper, the Princess told him what had happened to her. She had been carried away through a window of the royal castle by a powerful giant who was the lord of this castle and ruler over all the furry animals of the forest.

"Now I am his wife and though I don't regret it, I don't like being so alone all the time. That's why I'd be very glad if you could stay here with me, but I'm afraid for your sake. My husband went hunting this morning, and he could very well eat you, especially if he doesn't bring enough home for supper. He eats two dozen oxen at a sitting."

But the good Prince was not afraid. "Perhaps it won't be as bad as you think, sister," he said. "Since I'm already here, I'd like to meet your husband. Hide me somewhere here, so that I can have a look at him, and then in the morning, I'll be on my way again."

The youngest sister hid the Prince behind a row of hogsheads at the other end of the hall. No sooner had she done this when the door flew open and the giant walked in. He threw two dozen dead oxen on the table and said, "Here is my supper."

And then he took off his cape, which weighed a good ten hundred-weight, threw it over the hogsheads, and sat down at the table. "I'm tired, woman. Give me something to drink."

The youngest Princess took a cauldron, filled it with wine from the hogsheads, and set it in front of her husband. The giant fell upon it with both hands, lifted it to his lips, but when he sniffed the wine, he began to shout. "Woman, this wine reeks of man. Speak up! Who are you hiding here? Where is he? I want to see him, or there will be trouble!"

"Don't be so angry, my dear," said the youngest Princess tremulously. "It's only my brother, who has come to visit me. Do not harm him, I beg of you!"

23

The giant calmed down. "If it is your brother," he said, "then no harm shall come to him. Let him eat with us. We have food enough. But where is he? Show him to me!"

The youngest Princess went over to the hogsheads, took her brother by the hand and led him to the giant. He took an immediate liking to the Prince. "Your brother is a fine fellow, wife," he roared. "Never fear. I won't harm a hair on his head. Why, I know him already! I saw him only today in our woods."

Then the giant turned to the Prince. "Sit down, brother-in-law, have a drink of wine, and tell me how long you've been chasing that silver rabbit."

"For three days now," replied the Prince. "And tomorrow I shall go after it again, until I catch it."

"My dear fellow," said the giant, roaring with laughter, "so you intend to catch the silver rabbit! Remember me well: I have been chasing it now for ten years and I still haven't the slightest idea where it hides when it disappears like dust before my eyes. It would be better for you to stay here in peace with your sister and forget about the silver rabbit."

"No, brother-in-law," insisted the Prince, "I must try at least one more time before I give up."

"Very well," said the giant. "If that is what you wish, then I shall help you as much as I can. Here is a lock of golden hair. If you need something, it is enough to shake it, and I shall come to your assistance."

The Prince took the lock of golden hair, thanked the giant, and went to bed. Early the next morning they both set off, the giant as usual into his woods to hunt, and the Prince after the silver rabbit. He found it in the first pasture he came to and he chased after it all day, until at last they came out of the forest and found themselves on the shore of a blue sea. And just as the Prince was sure he had it, the silver rabbit hopped into the sea and ran over the water as if it were solid ground.

The poor Prince was at his wits' end, for he could not chase the rabbit across the water. Wondering where to go next, he looked around him, when suddenly he spied a poor little hut nestled among the rocks. The door of the hut was wide open, so he went inside.

The hut belonged to an old shoemaker. The Prince greeted him politely and said, "Tell me, good man, did you see a silver rabbit run past a while ago?"

The old shoemaker put a finger to his lips. "Shhh, young man, not so loud, I beg you. That's not a rabbit, as you think. It's a Princess, the daughter of the Persian King. I am her shoemaker, and every day I make her a new pair of shoes, and I take them to her palace myself."

The Prince was delighted with such good news. "And might I go there with you?" he asked.

"You might," replied the old shoemaker. "But you must never let anyone know it was I who took you there. As soon as I finish this new pair of shoes for the Princess, my flying cloak shall take us there. And so they won't find you in the castle right away, I'll give you this other cloak. All you have to do is throw it over your shoulders, and you'll be invisible."

As soon as the old man had finished the shoes for the Persian Princess, he gave the Prince one cloak, threw the other one across his shoulders, and then took the Prince upon his back. Instantly they rose up into the air and flew like the wind across the wide sea, right to the castle of the Persian King. And there, in the middle of the courtyard, they came to earth.

"And now, follow me," the old man said to the Prince, "and don't be afraid. As long as you have my cloak over your shoulders, no one can see you."

Sure enough, they walked through the whole castle until they came to the Princess's chambers and no one even noticed the Prince. The old shoemaker left the shoes for the Princess, and went out again. As for the Prince, he stayed behind to wait.

It wasn't long before the Princess herself returned. She was as beautiful as the day, but sad, and while she was still in the doorway, she said to her chambermaid, "I ran through the woods all day, but all in vain, for my loved one was not there today. Now I'm quite exhausted and very worried about him."

The chambermaid tried to cheer the Princess up. "Don't worry, your highness," she said, "for you will certainly see him again. And now you must eat and drink so you will have strength enough for tomorrow. Everything will be all right, you'll see."

And so the Princess ate and drank, but she didn't enjoy her meal as she usually did. Heavy with care, she went into her chambers.

The good Prince heard and saw everything, but because he was wearing the old man's magic cloak, no one could see him. He was ravenously hungry, and when he and the Princess were alone, he plucked up his courage and spoke.

"You have eaten, beautiful Princess, but I too am hungry and no one gave me anything."

The Princess was startled. "Who are you and where are you," she cried. "Why can I hear you but not see you?"

"Don't be frightened, beautiful Princess," replied the Prince. "I am the Prince you know so well. Look!"

And he threw off the old man's cloak. The Princess was overjoyed and she flung her arms around his neck and kissed him on the mouth. Then she called the chambermaid and had her bring food and drink and she entertained the Prince until daylight.

Next day the Princess had an audience with her father the Persian King. "My Royal Father," she said, "it is time I were married."

The old King was somewhat surprised. "And whomever do you wish to marry, daughter? Why, no one has asked me as yet for your hand."

But the Princess replied, "I have chosen a husband myself, Royal Father."

The King was even more astonished. "And where is he, my daughter? I should like to see him," he said.

"He is not far away, Royal Father," replied the Princess, "I shall bring him to you right away."

And then she ran to her chambers, took the Prince by the hand and led him to her father, the Persian King. "This is my chosen one, Royal Father," she said.

The old King took an instant liking to the Prince, and so he ordered a grand wedding celebration to be prepared for the next day, one befitting a Persian King who is giving his daughter in marriage.

And the wedding was a magnificent and joyous one, and after it was over, the Prince lived happily with his beautiful wife in the Persian King's castle. Only one thing marred their happiness. Even though they now belonged to each other, the Princess went out every morning and ran through the woods as a silver rabbit. And every morning before she left, she gave her husband the keys to all the rooms in the castle. The good Prince could go wherever he wished, even into the royal treasury. There was only one little room where he was not allowed to go.

"If you were to unlock it," the Princess warned him, "a great evil would befall us. But if you resist temptation for a year and a day, everything will be fine and I shall never more have to go into the woods."

The Prince found that time passed very slowly without the Princess. He spent his days walking through the gardens, looking through all the rooms and chambers and he saw so many beautiful and valuable things that he could scarcely believe his eyes. And so he was all the more curious about what could be in the forbidden room. For a long time, he did not dare to enter it, yet one day, his curiosity got the better of him. But no sooner had he opened the door to the forbidden room, than out jumped a demon. "Thank you, young man!" he shrieked. "Now your wife is mine forever. I'll take her away immediately!

The Prince was horrified, but he soon recovered his wits. "That's a fine reward for setting you free!" he said. "Couldn't you wait at least until noon tomorrow?"

"Well, all right," replied the demon. "Wait I shall but tomorrow at noon I'll take her away all the same."

And with that, he disappeared as though the earth had swallowed him up.

When the Princess returned that evening, the Prince looked so worried that she knew at once what had happened.

"I know what troubles you," she said. "You opened the door to the forbidden room and now I belong to the demon that was locked up inside."

The Prince nodded sadly. "Yes, my beautiful Princess, I made a mistake, and a grave one at that. But never fear. I shall save you, even from this demon."

The next day at precisely twelve o'clock the demon came rushing up to the castle and began pounding on the gate.

"Hey there, Prince," he shrieked, "where is your wife? I've come to get her."

The Prince was ready for him. "Right away, demon, if you'll just be patient a moment longer."

And then he put to his lips the ivory horn which his first brother-in-law had given him, and blew with all his might. No sooner had he done this than all the antlered animals came running from far and wide and began to butt and buffet the demon with their horns. It wasn't long before the demon cried out for a truce until the following day.

"Very well," said the Prince, "come tomorrow."

The next day at noon the demon appeared before the castle and once again pounded on the gate. "Hey there, Prince, here I am!" he cried. "Where is your wife?"

The Prince was ready for him.

"I'll be with you in a moment, demon," he said.

And then he placed to his lips the bird's beak which his second brother-in-law had given him, and he whistled with all his might. No sooner had he done this than all the birds from far and wide flew in and began to peck and claw at the demon. It wasn't long before the demon once again cried out for a truce until the following day.

"So be it," said the Prince. "But this is the last time."

At noon on the third day the demon beat on the castle gate a third time. "Hey there, Prince, here I am," he shouted. "Where is the Princess?"

The Prince was ready for him again. "I won't be a moment, demon," he said.

And then he pulled from his pocket the lock of golden hair his third brother-in-law had given him and he shook it with all his might. No sooner had he done this than furry animals came running up from far and wide and began to scratch and bite the demon. It wasn't long before the demon began to cry out for mercy. But this time the Prince did not give in, and he did not call off the wild animals until the demon lay helpless on the ground. Then it was easy for the Prince's men to bind him in irons and throw him into the fire. It is true that fire cannot harm a demon, but he can feel the pain like anyone else, and so he howled and shrieked as if he were being stuck with a pitch-fork. But the Prince did not relent, and ignored the demon's cries of agony. It wasn't until he promised to give up his claim to the Persian Princess for ever, and sealed that promise with his own blood, that the Prince ordered his men to release him. The devil leaped out of the fire and disappeared into the very depths of hell, and never showed himself in the Persian Kingdom again.

And now the Princess was at last truly free. She no longer had to run through the woods every day as a silver rabbit, and the Prince no longer had to wander alone through the castle and its chambers. From that moment on, he never left his beautiful wife's side and so they lived together happily and contentedly ever after.

WHEN WILLIE WOKE UP NEXT MORNING, he couldn't be sure whether everything that happened last night was real, or just a dream. So he was impatient for the evening and darkness to come, when Granny would close the door behind her and he would be alone with the crackling fire. When Granny's footsteps finally stopped in the kitchen below, he quickly sat down on the bear-skin rug in front of the fireplace to watch the fiery little men. It wasn't long before he began to see the spots in front of his eyes again. He had to rub his eyes, and when he opened them, the little girl from yesterday evening was sitting on the hearth.

"Well, Willie," she said, "shall we play?"

And so once more they played tag, hide-and-seek, and then, as before, they sat down by the fire. For a while the little girl made her lively little figures, and in no time at all she had made a whole swarm of them, but when they began to run off in all directions, she blew on them and they became a pile of ashes once more.

"Read me something again," she said.

So Willie obediently went and fetched Granny's books, showed her the pictures in them for a while, and then he chose a story and began to read. And this is what he read.

THE BRAVE LITTLE TAILOR
AND SEVEN AT A BLOW

Once there was a little tailor who was all jokes and jests and could always be relied upon for a bit of fun. All day he would sit in his little workshop, making his needle and thread fairly fly as he worked, and all the while he would sing at the top of his voice. Everyone who walked past would stop in for a chat, and the little tailor had a friendly word for everyone.

And that was just about all he did have, for otherwise, the tailor was as poor as a churchmouse. Though he worked diligently from morn till night, the village was a poor one and his work brought him scarcely enough to buy a piece of dry bread and a jug of milk. More than once, the tailor said to himself that he ought to give up tailoring and set off into the world to seek his fortune, but there was always something that wanted finishing, a coat or a pair of trousers he had promised someone to make, and so he sat in his little workshop and worked on.

One morning, just as he was getting ready to have breakfast, a farmer's wife went by his window on her way to market. She was carrying a pot of jam in a basket, and it smelled so good that the tailor couldn't help himself. He ran to the window with a piece of bread and said, "Good morning, good woman. What are you carrying that smells so delicious?"

The farmer's wife stopped and said, "I'm taking jam to market, master tailor. Would you like a taste?"

And without another word she spread some of her delectable jam on his slice of dry bread.

The tailor thanked the farmer's wife, put the slice of bread on the table and went into the next room for a cup of milk. By the time he returned, a swarm of flies had settled on the bread and begun feasting on the jam. When the little tailor saw this, he flew into

29

a rage. "I'll teach you miserable little beggars to steal my jam!" he shouted. And he gave them such a blow with a fly-swatter that everything trembled and shook. When he lifted the swatter, seven flies lay dead on the table.

"Seven at a blow," cried the tailor proudly. "A blow the like of which the world has never seen!" And he began to dance a little jig from sheer joy.

And then he had an idea: he should let everyone in the world know about his valiant deed. He took his scissors, he took his needle and thread and immediately set about making himself a beautiful belt, and on the belt, in big, bold colours, he stitched the words "Seven at a Blow!"

"And now I shall set off into the world," the little tailor decided and he began to make ready for the journey at once. He fixed his belt around his waist, set a cap upon his head, and thrust a couple of pieces of cheese into his knapsack so he wouldn't get hungry. He even slipped his little goldfinch into his pocket so that it wouldn't die of hunger in its cage by the window. Finally, he took his walking-stick and set off.

And so the tailor set off and marched briskly down the road away from the village, as though the thunder itself were pounding at his heels. About noon he found himself at the foot of some high mountains far from his village. And there, right in the middle of the road, a very strange thing made him stop short.

"If it weren't so big," said the good tailor, shaking his head, "I'd say it was a boot."

"And here's another one," he cried, as soon as he had looked around him. And when he raised his eyes higher and yet higher, he saw that they really were boots, and that above them soared a pair of knees, and above the knees a huge stomach thrust out, and above the stomach stretched a pair of broad shoulders, and above the shoulders towered a head.

In short, before the tailor was standing a giant as big as a mountain and he was looking somewhere into the distance.

But the little tailor was not afraid of him. "Hallo up there," he shouted with all his might so the giant could hear him. "How would you like to go into the world with me?"

The giant looked down at his feet to see what was making the strange noise, and then he roared with laughter. "Well, well, well, you're a daring little pip-squeak, aren't you?"

But the tailor didn't lose heart. "Watch who you call a pip-squeak," he retorted. "I have the strength of seven. Just look!"

And he showed the giant his belt.

The giant was not the fastest of readers, but even so he managed to read what the tailor had sewn there syllable by syllable. Then he shook his head and said, "Very well then, if you're so strong, let's have a contest. And if you make a good showing of yourself, I'll take you home to meet my brother."

"Agreed," said the tailor. "We'll see who's the stronger."

The giant didn't wait to be asked twice. He picked up a rock from the road and squeezed it so hard that it crumbled into dust in his fist.

But the little tailor only laughed. "That's nothing. I can squeeze harder than that."

And then he bent over, as though he were looking for a stone, but at the same time he secretly drew one of the lumps of cheese out of his knapsack and squeezed it so hard that the whey ran out of it.

The giant was astounded. Squeezing water from a stone was something he truly could not do.

"All right," he grumbled, "if you're so strong, let's try again."

And he picked up another rock from the road and threw it into the air so high that it took an hour for it to fall back to earth again.

But again the little tailor only laughed. "That's nothing. I can.throw higher than that."

And he bent over, as though he were looking for a stone, but at the same time he secretly drew the little goldfinch from his pocket and threw it into the air. They waited an hour, and another hour, but naturally, the goldfinch didn't fall back to earth. It was glad to be free and had flown off, never to return.

The giant was astonished for truly, he could not throw a stone into the air so high that it would stay up for more than two hours.

"All right," he grumbled, "if you're so strong, we'll try one more time. If you can help me carry that uprooted oak-tree home, we'll be friends forever."

And he pointed to a huge oak-tree which lay by the edge of the woods.

But the little tailor only laughed again. "That's nothing. I can carry even more than that. You take the trunk, and I'll carry the crown and the branches. That's the heavier part."

The gullible giant grasped the oak by the trunk, threw it over his shoulder, and set off. As soon as his back was turned, the little tailor climbed nimbly into the branches dragging along the ground and there he sat, as comfortable as a king. From time to time he would pant heavily, as though he were carrying the whole oak-tree himself, and he would urge the giant on and scold him for not carrying his share of the weight.

At last they came to the cave where the giant lived with his brother. The giant threw the tree down with a great crash by the mouth of the cave, and then sat down up on it. He was puffing so hard he could scarcely catch his breath, but the little tailor only laughed, and said "Why didn't you tell me you were so exhausted? I could have carried the whole tree myself. If I can lay low seven at a blow a tree like that is child's play!"

The giant was astonished, for he simply couldn't carry an oak-tree that big without puffing and panting.

"All right," he said, "come and meet my brother. I'll wager you've never met a fellow like him in your life before."

And he led the little tailor into the cave where another giant was sitting roasting two oxen over a fire. He welcomed the little tailor politely, shook his head when he heard of his great strength, and gave him a generous helping of roast ox for supper. Then they gave him a bed on a pile of dry leaves in the corner. The little tailor snuggled into the leaves and pretended to fall asleep, but as soon as the giants were asleep beside him, he slipped out of his bed and lay down under the table instead, leaving only his knapsack and coat in the leaves.

Towards morning, both the giants woke up and speaking in whispers, they decided to tickle their guest a little with a club.

31

"If he's such a strong fellow," they laughed, "he'll hardly feel a thing." And together they fell upon the empty coat and knapsack in the leaves with their clubs. Thinking that was the end of the tailor, they went down to the brook to wash. But the tailor was unharmed. He walked out of the cave and as soon as the poor giants caught sight of him, they took to their heels and fled, shouting, "Now we're doomed. Now he'll beat both of us to death!"

But the little tailor just stood and watched them run away, and then he set off to seek further adventures.

The road took him to the royal town. Just outside its gates, he sat down under a flowering linden tree, and because he was somewhat exhausted, he pulled his cap over his eyes and was soon sound asleep. When he woke up, the King himself was standing over him. He had set off on his afternoon ride and as they were going by the flowering linden, the motto on the tailor's belt caught his eye.

"Seven at a blow?" said the King in amazement, halting his horse. "I could use a strong fellow like that."

And so when the tailor awoke, the King asked him if he would like to enter his service.

"And why not your majesty?", said the tailor. "I have set out into the world to seek my fortune, and perhaps I'll find it right here with you."

And so the little tailor entered the service of the King. The King thought the world of him. He gave him a nice house of his own and a pouch of ducats, and named him Commander of his Personal Guard. Naturally the King's officers were displeased.

"Who knows whether a wanderer like that really killed seven at a blow or not," they complained to the King.

At first the King dismissed their complaints, but then he decided to test the tailor after all. One morning he summoned the little tailor and said, "Listen, I have something for you to do. In the woods behind our castle there is a wild boar who has been wreaking havoc in our royal gardens, and who gores everyone he meets. If you will rid me of him you shall have anything you wish, even my daughter's hand in marriage. But if you fail, I do not wish to lay eyes on you again."

Everyone expected the little tailor to walk away in despair but he merely laughed and said, "If it's nothing worse than that, your majesty, then order the wedding to be prepared. Tomorrow I shall have a look at that wild boar. If I can lay low seven at a blow, then I can lay him low as well."

And sure enough, first thing next morning, the little tailor set out to find the terrible wild boar. He found it easily enough, for the boar was furiously rooting up a rose bush by an old chapel just outside the royal gardens. As soon as it saw the tailor, it lifted its head, grunted, and charged after him. But the stout-hearted little tailor was not afraid. He ran as fast as his legs would carry him straight for the chapel. The door of the chapel was open, but instead of running inside, the little tailor jumped nimbly to one side just as he reached the entrance and the wild boar flew through the open door into the chapel. Before it could stop, turn around and run out again, the tailor had slammed the door shut and locked it firmly. Then, slipping the key into his pocket, he hurried off gaily to his master.

"The wild boar is trapped," he said to the King," "and here is the key to the trap. You may send for it, and then prepare the wedding."

The King was glad to be rid of the bothersome beast, but he was in no hurry to have the wedding just yet. "We shall have the wedding soon enough," he said, "but before I give you my daughter, I have another task for you. Over there in those woods there lives an evil old unicorn who destroys the crops throughout the kingdom. If anyone tries to stop him he runs him through with that horn of his. If you will get rid of this unicorn for us, not only will there be a wedding, but you shall receive half my kingdom as well. But if you fail, never show yourself to me again."

Everyone expected the little tailor to gather up his belongings and leave, but he merely laughed and said, "If it's nothing worse than that, your majesty, then order the wedding to be prepared at once. I shall have a look at this unicorn tomorrow. If I can do away with seven at a blow, I can do away with him too!"

And sure enough, first thing next morning, the little tailor set off into the woods to look for the unicorn. He wasn't hard to find, for wherever he went, he left a trail of broken trees and destruction behind him. Only the huge old oak trees were too much for him, and it was by just such a tree that the little tailor came upon the unicorn. As soon as the unicorn saw him, he lifted his head, whinneyed, and charged straight at him. But the brave little tailor was not afraid. He stood his ground, and waited until the unicorn was running as fast as he could and then at the very last moment, he jumped aside. Instead of running down the tailor, the unicorn struck the tree at full speed with his one horn, and it stuck so fast that he couldn't pull it out. The tailor cut off the unicorn's tail and hurried to the King.

"The unicorn is trapped, your majesty," he said. "Here is his tail. You may send someone for him and then prepare the wedding."

The King was glad to have the unicorn out of the way, but he was in no hurry, even now, to have the wedding. "It won't be long now, but before I give you my daughter and half my kingdom, I have one last task for you. Over there, in those mountains live two giants and these giants are the terror of my whole realm. They rob and murder and no one is safe from them, not even myself and my daughter. If you will rid us of them, my daughter and my throne are yours. If you fail, however, never show yourself here again."

Everyone expected that this time little tailor would surely give up and leave. But he merely laughed and said, "If it's nothing worse than that, your majesty, then order the wedding to be prepared at once. Tomorrow I shall go and have a look at these giants. Why I believe I even know them. If I can kill seven at a blow, I can kill them too."

And sure enough, first thing next morning the little tailor set off into the mountains to find the giants. About noon, he came to the edge of the forest, jumped down from his horse, and continued on foot. It wasn't long before he was at their cave. Both giants had just had their lunch and were sleeping in the grass beside a spreading oak, and snoring so loudly the trees around shook. But the little tailor was not afraid. He filled his pockets with stones and very quietly, he climbed up the oak-tree. When he reached the top, he threw a stone down at one of the giants. His aim was good, and he hit the giant right on the nose. The giant jumped up as if something had stung him, looked all around, and then shouted gruffly at his brother, "Hey, why did you punch me in the nose? Why don't you let me sleep?"

"I didn't punch you in the nose," grumbled the second giant, "You must have been dreaming. Go back to sleep, and let me sleep too."

The first giant was satisfied, rolled over on his other side and in a little while both were sound asleep again and the trees shook with their snoring. But the little tailor didn't let them sleep for long. He took another stone and threw it at the second giant. His aim was true, and he hit him full in the ear. The giant jumped up, as if someone had stabbed him, looked around, and then shouted at his brother, "Hey, why did you punch me in the ear? Why can't you let me sleep?"

"I didn't punch you in the ear," growled the first giant. "You must have been dreaming. Go back to sleep and leave me alone."

The second giant was satisfied with this, rolled over on his other side and in a little while both of them were sound asleep once more and the trees shook with their snoring. But the little tailor didn't let them sleep for long. He took two stones this time and threw them at both the giants at once. His aim was faultless once more and he struck both of them right on the forehead.

Both giants leaped up as if someone had stuck them with a pitchfork, and they started in at each other.

"Why did you hit me on the forehead?"

"I didn't hit you, you hit me!"

"It was you who hit me!"

"Me? It was you!"

Word followed upon word, blow upon blow and soon both giants reached for their clubs and they beat each other, so long that at last both of them lay lifeless on the ground under the oak tree. And now it was a simple matter for the tailor to cut off their heads and carry them to the King.

"The giants are dead, your majesty," he said. "And here are their heads. Now you may send for their treasure, and then prepare the wedding. Really and truly this time."

The King was glad to be rid of the giants and whether he wanted to or not there was nothing to do but arrange a magnificent royal wedding. And so the little tailor took the Princess as his wife, and because the King had no son, he became heir to the throne. No one suspected that the King's heir was once a poor tailor. No one knew that he once sewed coats and trousers for the poor people of his village. And naturally the tailor wasn't about to tell anyone. But one night, he dreamed that he was in his workshop again, and in his sleep, he cried aloud to his assistant, "Hey there, you, sew the patch on those trousers properly!"

The tailor spoke so loudly that he woke the Princess. For a while she listened to what her husband was saying in his sleep and then she burst into tears. "Who have I married?" she wept. "He's no hero, just a common tailor who sews patches on trousers."

The Princess wept and carried on so long that she woke up her husband. When he heard the Princess weeping, he immediately guessed that he had given himself away, but he kept this to himself, and merely turned over, pretending to be still asleep

In the morning, the Princess ran to tell her father the King what kind (
husband really was. The King's brow furrowed in anger. "If it is as you say
get rid of this man for you. When he goes to sleep tonight, open the bed-cl
and my guard will chop off his head."

But the little tailor was prepared for just such a thing. No sooner had h
than he began to snore, as though he were sound asleep, and he waited for s
happen. In a while, the Princess got quietly out of bed and opened the doo
the guard could enter the bed-chamber, the little tailor turned over, as tho
dreaming again and began to shout, "Here I come. Take that! I'll kill sevei
a blow. Seven at a blow!"

The King's guard thought that he was shouting at them. They threw
swords, threw down their shields, and took to their heels as though the
beneath their feet were on fire. They didn't stop until they came to the woo
never showed themselves in the royal castle again. Even the King was afra
one day the little tailor were to go after him too?

"'t would be better," he said, "to give him my crown and sceptre myself.'
had the brave little tailor crowned as his successor.

And that is how a poor village tailor finally became ruler over a whole ki
ruled wisely, his subjects loved him and his enemies feared him. And so they
too, for was he not a King who had killed seven at a blow? Such a King ha
reigned since the world began. Even the Princess herself had to admit that,
she grew to be very fond of the tailor, even though he said strange things i
And so they lived together in love and harmony happily ever after.

THE TALE WAS OVER. The little girl lay on the bear-skin rug by the hearth and her eyes were closed as though she were sleeping. But she wasn't, for as soon as Willie finished reading, she wanted to hear another story. But Willie also wanted to close his eyes and listen. So he said, "Why don't you tell a story now?"

"I know what you want," she laughed, and her laughter sounded like little bells. "All right then, listen."

And as soon as she raised her finger to her lips, he heard a sound like someone singing in the chimney, and the still, quiet voice of the Wind began to speak. And this is the story she told.

THE SHAH, THE VIZIER,
AND THE DERVISH

Once upon a time, long ago, there lived a Shah. He was very wealthy, and had a beautiful palace full of magnificent treasures, but the greatest treasure of all was his beautiful wife. The Shah loved her more than anything else in the world and his wife returned his affection with love just as faithful and true. But those who have love and good fortune are often victims of the envy of others, and this Shah, powerful as he was, was no exception. In his court, there was a certain Vizier, who was a man with a heart as black as night. In the depths of his soul, he longed after the throne of his master and the love of his master's beautiful wife.

He showed nothing of his envy, of course, because he knew he would be rewarded with death, but secretly, he thought of nothing else day and night except how to make his evil dream come true.

And it happened that one day, a dervish arrived in the royal town. He had wandered through the world for many years, and had seen much and learned a great deal. When he began to perform in the market-place, the people were astonished and amazed at his tricks. Soon the whole town was talking about him, and it wasn't long before the Shah himself heard about the dervish and his wonderful magic. He sent for his Vizier and told him, "Go and see what kind of man this dervish is, and what he wants here."

The Vizier went into town, inquired of various people, went to watch the dervish perform, and then returned to his master.

"Oh Shah," he said, "this dervish knows several fine tricks, and he performs them for people to earn his daily bread." The Shah enjoyed such amusements, and so he commanded the Vizier, "Go and bring him to me. Let him perform for me as well."

The Vizier went into the town a second time, sought out the dervish and brought him before the Shah. The Shah was quite impressed by the dervish's performance, but, wishing to see something even better, he said, "These tricks of yours are nothing at all out of the ordinary, Dervish! I have seen similar things many times. Can't you do something better?"

The dervish was hurt that the Shah had not liked his magic, but he did not let him see it. Instead he bowed deeply, and said, "Oh Shah, if you wish to see something better, command all those present to leave, and then I shall show you something you have never seen before, and will never see again as long as you live."

The Shah was curious to know what magic the dervish was about to show him, and he commanded the room to be cleared. As soon as they were alone, the dervish said, "And now, Oh Shah, I shall perform a feat of magic which I alone know how to do. I shall leave my body and enter another. Have a chicken brought in."

The Shah clapped for servants and commanded them to bring a chicken. As soon as the servants had left, the dervish took the chicken, wrung its neck, and lay its dead body at the Shah's feet. Then he made a secret sign with his hand and stepped out of his body. The Shah could scarcely believe his eyes. For all at once, the dervish's body lay on the floor as if dead and in the very same moment, the chicken came alive and began to cluck and strut about.

After a while, the dervish left the chicken and returned to his own body. The chicken collapsed at the Shah's feet and was dead once more, while the dervish rose alive and hearty and bowed deeply to the Shah.

"Tell me, Oh Shah, have you ever seen such magic before?" he asked.

The Shah had to admit that he hadn't, and at once he began to persuade the dervish to teach him the trick. At first, the dervish was reluctant but finally he nodded. "I will do so, Oh Shah, but you must be careful, for one day you may regret it."

But the Shah insisted. "Why should I regret it !" he asked. "Just teach me how to do it, and you shall receive a jug full of gold."

Now a jug of gold is not a great deal for such powerful magic, but the dervish was poor, and had to be content with it, and the same day he taught the Shah his trick. That very night, the Shah sent him the jug of gold in secret, so that no one would know about it, not even the Vizier.

The Shah wanted to conceal his magic powers from everyone, but he couldn't keep it a secret from the Vizier. For so often did he leave his body and enter the body of other people and animals, that the Vizier finally found out.

"Only that dervish could have taught the Shah such magic," he said to himself, and the same night he sent for him secretly. When the dervish had bowed deeply before him, the Vizier came right to the point.

"I know what it is you have taught our Shah," he said, "and I wish to learn this magic too. If you will teach me, I shall give you whatever you ask."

The dervish let him plead a little longer, and then said, "I will teach you this trick too, O Vizier, but only if you give me your daughter's hand in marriage."

Now the Vizier had a very beautiful daughter and the poor dervish had seen her once and from that moment on he could think of nothing else. She was the only reason he had remained in the town, and the only reason he had come when the Vizier summoned him.

When the Vizier heard what the dervish wanted, he very nearly called his guard. But then he disguised his anger behind a sweet smile and nodded. "She shall be yours, Dervish. Only allow me to make your wish known to her and hear her answer."

Then he went to his daughter's chambers and told her what had happened and who desired her hand in marriage. The Vizier's daughter was quite upset. "I shall not take any wandering dervish for a husband, father. You cannot wish this of me. Tell him that if he desires the Vizier's daughter as his wife, he must, according to the custom, bring her a jug of gold as a wedding gift."

The Vizier was pleased with his daughter's answer. "You are extremely clever, my daughter!" he said. "Where would a poor dervish get a jug of gold! I shall go and give him your reply."

And with that, he returned to the dervish and told him what his daughter had said. "If you desire her as your wife, you must bring her a jug of gold as a gift. Such is the custom here."

The Vizier expected the dervish to be put to shame. Imagine his surprise when the dervish replied, "If that is the custom, then she shall have the jug of gold this very evening."

The Vizier saw that he must try a different approach, and so he said, "Very well, send for the jug, and when it arrives, you will teach me your magic. Then you shall receive what belongs to you."

The poor dervish sent for the jug of gold and the very same day he taught the Vizier his magic. But when he wanted to take away his daughter, the Vizier stopped him "Just a moment, Dervish. Things can't be done in such a hurry. After all, I am the Vizier of the Shah himself. I must announce the marriage to the people, make the proper preparations, and wait forty days. That is the custom here."

But such a custom was not to the dervish's taste. He wanted to take his beautiful bride away with him immediately, and when the Vizier refused, the dervish made such a fuss and commotion that the Vizier finally called in his guard and had the poor bridegroom driven out of the house. But he did not return the jug of gold, and the dervish had to be content to escape with his life. He ran away from the town into the woods.

While the poor dervish was wandering about somewhere in the forest, the treacherous Vizier was waiting for the right moment. He did not have to wait long. One day, the Shah invited him to come along on the hunt. The Vizier and the Shah rode off together alone after a gazelle, and when they had killed it, the Vizier dismounted and went over to the dead animal.

"I am well aware, Oh Shah, that you possess more than a few magic powers, but I'll wager that I know some you have never heard of. Watch!"

43

And without another word he left his own body and entered the body of the dead gazelle. The gazelle instantly came to life, while the Vizier's body lay on the ground as if dead. It wasn't until the Vizier once again returned to his own body that it came alive again and the gazelle once more sunk to the grass, dead. The Vizier bowed deeply before the Shah and said, "That magic was taught to me by a wandering dervish, and there is no one else in the world except the two of us who know it."

"Oh, but there is," said the Shah, not wishing to be humiliated. "Just watch!"

And without wasting another moment, he entered the body of the gazelle himself, while his own body remained lifeless in the grass. This was just what the treacherous Vizier had been waiting for. He quickly left his own body and stepped into the body of his master, leaving his own lying on the ground. Then he leapt into the Shah's horse and galloped away to the nearest village.

When the villagers saw the Shah himself approaching they fell on their faces before him. The Vizier in the Shah's body spoke to them. "Go into the woods," he commanded. "There you will find the body of my Vizier. We were out hunting together and suddenly he fell to the ground and was dead. Take his body to the town and give it to his relations."

The villagers did as they were commanded, and took the Viziers' lifeless body to his family. His wife and children mourned him for three days and three nights, and then they buried him with full honours. But no one knew that the Vizier had not died at all and was living on in the Shah's body.

Not even the Shah's beautiful wife knew this. Towards evening, when the guard announced that the Shah was returning from the hunt, she ran joyfully to watch the arrival of her beloved lord and master through the latticed window of her chamber. The Shah jumped down from his horse, nodded graciously to his servants who were on their faces before him, and began to walk straight for the harem. The Shah's beautiful wife ran out to meet him, but when she was half-way there, she stopped short. The man who was walking towards her had the Shah's face, and even the Shah's body and attire, but his eyes were not the same, and his voice was strange.

"That is not my beloved master," she said to herself. "It is someone else in his shape."

And without a word she turned round and locked herself in her room.

The Vizier in the Shah's body had not expected such a welcome. After all he had gone through to gain the Shah's beautiful wife, and now the lovely lady had run away from him! Bitterly, he went to his chambers and contented himself with the knowledge that at least he possessed the Shah's throne.

While the treacherous Vizier in the Shah's body luxuriated on the throne, the Shah in the gazelle's body fled swiftly over mountain and across valley. He was afraid that the Vizier or his men might try to kill him, and so he ran as long as his strength would carry him until he came to a deep forest on the very edge of his empire. There he stopped to rest, and as luck would have it he saw a dead parrot under a nearby tree. Without a moment's delay, the Shah stepped into its body and the parrot flew happily away to join a flock of its comrades.

And so for a time the Shah lived among the parrots. One day, however, a fowler came into the forest. As soon as the Shah saw him, he warned the other parrots. "Be very careful," he said. "That man is a fowler. He will set traps and try to catch you. You must fly away from here as fast as you can!"

The parrots took the advice of their wise friend and flew away to another wood. The Shah, however, did not leave with them but instead flew down to the ground and let the fowler catch him.

The fowler rejoiced to have caught such a beautiful parrot, but his joy was no greater than the Shah's. For the Shah had recognized that he was the wandering dervish who had once taught him the magic. He did not let on that he knew him, however, but merely asked, "If you wish to become rich quickly, fowler, take me to the Shah's town and sell me to the Shah himself. The Shah will give you a hundred pieces of gold for me, you'll see."

This piece of advice appealed to the fowler, and he said, "You're right, parrot, I shall go there, sell you to the Shah, and if the proper moment comes, I shall complain to him of the injustice his Vizier did me. Perhaps he will give me a hearing."

And then he told the parrot what the evil Vizier had done and how he had been badly treated at his hands. The parrot listened to all this, and then said. "You may try it, fowler, but be careful. Think well before you speak. Not everyone who looks like the Shah and wears the Shah's clothing is the Shah."

"You are right, parrot," said the fowler. "I shall watch my tongue."

And so the fowler went to the royal town and threw himself in the dust before the Shah. The Shah liked the parrot immediately. "Stand, fowler," he said, "and tell me how much you would like for this parrot."

"A hundred pieces of gold, O Shah," replied the fowler, lifting his face from the ground. But as soon as he looked into the Shah's face, he saw at once that it was not the real Shah. He had the Shaw's features, he had the Shaw's body and clothing, but his eyes and his voice were different. And so he thought it better not to mention the injustice at all. He accepted the purse of gold, bowed silently and was gone. But he did not leave the town, for he was curious to see what would happen next.

While the fowler was waiting in the town, the Shah's wife consoled herself with the parrot. The Vizier in the Shah's body had sent her the bird as a gift, and it made her very happy. The Shah himself was even happier to see his dear wife after such a long time. But not even the parrot could make her gay for long. She played with him for a while, but soon her melancholy thoughts overcame her once more. When the parrot saw this, he spoke and said, "Why are you so sad and melancholy, fair lady?"

And the Shah's beautiful wife sighed and said, "I'd rather you wouldn't ask, parrot. My heart is so full of grief that I can speak to no one about it."

But the parrot would not be put off, and said, "Please tell me about it, fair lady. Perhaps I can help you."

And the Shah's beautiful wife gave in and said, "I was deeply fond of my lord and master, the Shah. But some time ago he was out hunting with his Vizier, and when he returned from the hunt, he was quite a different person. His face was that of my master's, and his body and his attire were the same, but his eyes and his voice were different. Since that time, I have been afraid of him and I run whenever I see him. Most of the time I feel like running away for good."

When the parrot heard this, his heart leapt for joy. He perched on her hand, looked into her eyes, and said, "Look at me, listen well to my voice, and tell me if you recognize it."

The Shah's beautiful wife looked into the parrot's eyes, listened to his kind voice for a while, and then cried joyously, "Your eyes are the eyes of my master, and your voice is the voice of our Shah himself!"

And the parrot flapped his wings with delight and said, "And I am the Shah. I am your husband."

And then he told his beloved wife all that had happened and all that he had gone through. The Shah's beautiful wife listened, and then burst into tears.

"But what shall we do now? What ever will become of us, my lord?"

The parrot soothed his dear wife. "Now, now there's nothing to be afraid of. Listen carefully. When the false Shah comes to you today, be kind and loving to him. Then he will ask you why you have been so unkind to him this past while, and you must reply that you do not even know yourself, but since the day he returned from the hunt, he seemed to be quite different and strange, as if he were hiding something from you. He will say that he is hiding nothing from you, and then you tell him to show you the magic trick he learned from that wandering dervish. At first he will not want to, but in the end, he will give in. And when he does, everything will be well again, you'll see."

The parrot advised his beautiful wife well. For a long time, the treacherous Vizier did not want to reveal his magic trick, but when he saw tears in the eyes of the Shah's wife, he softened and said, "Very well, my wife, I shall show you the magic trick. Have a dog brought in, have it killed, and then send your servants out."

The Shah's beautiful wife did as she was told. The dog was brought in, killed, and then all the servants were sent away. Only the parrot remained with them in the room.

The Vizier in the Shah's body made a secret sign with his hand and whispered a magic word, as the wandering dervish had taught him, and then stepped out of his own body and into the body of the dead dog. And this was the moment the Shah had been waiting for. He left the parrot, returned to his own body, and then said, "Listen to what I have to tell you, Vizier. You betrayed me shamefully, like a dog, and a dog you shall remain for the rest of your days!"

And he drove the Vizier in the body of a mangy dog from the palace. In his place, he called the poor dervish, made him his Vizier, and gave him the hand of the Vizier's beautiful daughter in marriage. And then he lived in love with his beautiful wife and ruled over his people wisely and justly ever after, because he knew himself what injustice and suffering was, and how sweet is love and fidelity. At least, this is what the tale of the Shah, the Vizier and the dervish tells us.

WILLIE WAS STILL NOT CERTAIN whether it was all just a dream or not. All morning, he hung around his grandmother not knowing whether to ask her but finally he did.

"Granny, what's that singing in the chimney every night?"

"Why it's just the wind," replied Granny.

Willie hesitated a while before asking his next question. "And does the wind have children?"

"That's something I can't tell you, child," she replied. "But why shouldn't it have?"

But she smiled so strangely when she said it that Willie was quite confused.

Even so, the little girl came again that evening. She was sitting on the bear-skin rug in front of the fire even before Willie managed to climb out of bed, where Granny had tucked him in.

For a little while they played tag and hide-and-seek very quietly so Granny wouldn't find them out. Then the little girl made her little figures and animals. Willie would like to have kept just one but as soon as he touched them, they immediately turned to ash once more.

"Your fingers are too strong," laughed the little girl. "Read me something instead."

And she blew all the figures away in a little cloud of dust.

Willie let the book fall open where it would and began to read slowly and clearly. And this is what he read.

THE KING WHO COULD WEAVE STRAW MATS

Once upon a time, there was a young King, as sturdy as a pine tree and as handsome as a flower, in short, a joy to behold, and this King was a keen hunter. Whenever he had the time, he mounted his horse and set off at gallop for the woods with his huntsmen, the dogs and the falcons not far behind.

Once, while out hunting, the young King put up a beautiful doe. The doe fled swiftly before the huntsmen, but the King was not easily discouraged and urged his horse after her. For a long time, he followed her while the deer ran as fast as her legs would take her until at last, she ran out of the woods into a flowering meadow. And there, she miraculously disappeared, as though she had taken refuge in the little cottage which stood there in the shade of a high oak-tree.

The young King brought his horse to a halt by the cottage gate, jumped out of the saddle, and was about to enter when suddenly he froze in his steps. On the doorstep of the cottage stood a maiden so beautiful that she took the young King's breath away.

As soon as the King saw her he forgot at once about the deer, the hunt and everything else, and could only stand and stare at the girl. Finally he found his tongue and asked, "Who are you, fair maid?"

"I'm the woodsman's daughter, noble sir," the maiden replied boldly.

But the King wanted to know more. "And what do they call you?" he asked. "They call me Sylvia," she replied boldly.

And for a third time the King asked, "And wouldn't you like to be my wife, beautiful Sylvia?"

Sylvia looked the King up and down from head to foot, and then said, "First I would have to know who you are."

The young King was astonished. "You mean you don't know who I am? Why, I am the King of this country!"

But Sylvia had never heard of the King, nor of any kings. "King?" she asked. "And what do you do? What is your trade?"

The young King was even more amazed. "What do I do? Why, I rule, and therefore I need no trade."

But Sylvia would not be convinced. "I will marry no man who has no trade. If you wish me to be your wife, come for me when you learn a decent craft!"

And so the young King returned from the hunt downcast and sorrowful. He was suffering the pangs of love and desire, and when they put down roots in the heart, nothing can pull them out again. So it was with the young King. His heart longed for the beautiful Sylvia, and he could think of nothing else but her and the miserable trade. How could he learn a trade as quickly as possible?

Finally he decided to summon all the craftsmen in the royal town to the castle, cabinetmakers, wheelwrights, carpenters, blacksmiths, painters, masons and who knows what else. When they were all assembled, the young King began to inquire.

"Tell me, masters," he said to them. "Which trade could I learn in the shortest possible time?"

The master craftsmen shook their heads. "In the shortest time, your majesty?" they replied. "That we cannot tell you. To learn carpentry would take a man at least three years."

"And so would cabinetmaking!"

"And so would blacksmithing!"

But this was much to long a time for the young King. "That is impossible, masters," he said. "I am looking for someone who could teach me his trade in two or three months!"

At this an old man asked to speak. "Your majesty, I can teach you a trade in three months," he said.

The King was overjoyed. "And what do you do, old man?" he asked.

"I make mats, and a fine trade it is, too," he answered. "Just send for some reeds, and you will see for yourself."

The young King ordered all the necessary materials to be sent and began to learn the matmaker's craft. It was not easy, but his fingers were nimble and within three months he had really and truly learned how to weave mats. When he had put the finishing touches to his masterpiece, he thanked the old man for his instruction, rewarded him handsomely, and set off into the woods to meet his beloved Sylvia.

"Here I am at last, Sylvia," he said. "I have come for you!"

But first Sylvia wanted to know if he had done as she had asked. "Have you learned a trade?" she inquired.

"I have," replied the King. "I can weave straw mats."

Sylvia was satisfied. "That is good," she said.

"Now you will weave mats, and I shall take them to market and we will have enough to live on till the end of our lives."

But the King did not want to weave mats for the rest of his life. "There is no need for that, Sylvia," he said. "After all, I am a King and I have enough of everything. I learned that trade only because of you. I shall never have to use it."

But Sylvia had her own ideas. "You never know! But if you say you are a King and have enough of everything, so be it. We shall be kings together then, and we shall leave your trade for a rainy day."

And so the young King took Sylvia to his castle and there he held a royal wedding. And it was then Sylvia knew for certain that her husband truly had enough of everything, for in all her life she had never even dreamed of such glory, magnificence and wealth.

But this tale does not end with the wedding. The King and his Queen lived together in happiness and contentment. Together, they ruled, together they made merry, and the only time they were apart was when the young King went hunting alone, as he had done before. One day, the good King came to say farewell to his wife and he said, "I am going hunting, Sylvia, and I shall remain in the woods three days and three nights. May all go well with you here, and think of me while I'm gone!"

The King set off and dear Sylvia waited for him in her chambers. The first day she waited and sang all day, the second day she waited and sighed all day. The third day she waited, and all at once she felt the sharp pain of worry in her heart, for the good King had not yet returned. He didn't come in the morning, he didn't come in the evening; he didn't even come at night.

And how could he, when robbers had taken him prisoner! On the very first day of the hunt, he became lost and at nightfall, he stopped at an inn. But a band of robbers had their den in this very inn, and they robbed any wayfarer who ever passed the night there. About midnight the leader of the robbers awakened the King with his sword drawn. "Who are you and what do you want here?" he hissed. "Speak, if your life is dear to you!"

Now the King had come to the inn dressed in common hunter's clothing and no one could recognize him for a gentleman, let alone a king. And so he replied, "I'm a hunter and I lost my way while out hunting."

But the leader of the robbers wanted to know more, "Have you a family who can pay your ransom?"

"I have no one!" replied the young King, "I am just a poor, solitary hunter!"

"Then you shall die," said the leader of the robbers.

But the King did not plead for mercy. "If I die," he answered, "so be it. But before I die, I may be of some use to you. I can weave beautiful mats."

The robbers burst into laughter.

"And what good will these mats of yours be to us?"

"Do not laugh," replied the King. "The Queen herself takes great pleasure in my mats, and buys them often. Take her one and you shall see for yourselves."

"Very well, we shall try it," decided the leader. "But woe unto you if what you say is not true! Now, what do you need?"

"Nothing more than a bundle of reeds and a little dye," replied the King.

The robbers brought the King what he needed, and he started to work. He prepared the reeds, dyed them different colours, and then began to weave a large, beautiful mat covered with ornaments and flowers of all kinds. Between these decorations he wove various letters, from which one could easily read where he was and what had happened to him.

When the mat was ready, he asked the robbers if any of them knew how to read and write.

The robbers burst into laughter. "What use would reading and writing be to us in the woods?"

The young King was greatly relieved, but he kept his joy to himself and with a serious face, he replied.

"Do not laugh! The Queen herself is from the woods, yet she can read. You will see how happy she will be when you show her my mat."

The robbers were also pleased with the mat. That same day the leader himself set out for the royal castle. Disguised as a merchant, he came before the Queen and bowed deeply.

"I have heard, your highness," he said, "that you are fond of beautiful mats. I have brought one for you to look at, should you wish to buy it."

The Queen had been sitting sadly at the window for four days now, looking in vain towards the woods from which her husband had still not returned. As soon as she heard the merchant mention the mat, she jumped up from her chair and said, "Show it to me, good man. If the mat is truly as beautiful as you say, you shall receive a purse of ducats."

The merchant unrolled the mat and the Queen was overjoyed, for she saw at once who had made it, and she knew at once what had happened to her dear husband. She could read it all in the mat. But she let out nothing to the merchant.

"You were right, good man," was all she said. "This mat of yours is lovely indeed. Here is your purse of ducats. Come again soon!"

The leader of the robbers took the purse and hurried back to the inn in the woods. The same day, the King had to begin a second mat for the Queen.

But he never finished it. As soon as the merchant had disappeared into the woods, good Sylvia summoned the King's best regiment and sent them to the robbers' inn. They arrived at midnight, just when the robbers were in the middle of a wild celebration. When the soldier's burst in on them, they were so petrified they did not even try to defend themselves. In the twinkling of an eye they were all bound and the King was free. He hurried to embrace his dear wife.

"Thank you, Sylvia. You have saved my life," he said joyfully.

But the good Queen just laughed. "It was not I who saved your life, but your trade. Even though you may belittle it, you cannot deny that it came in useful to you."

The King saw that he had married a woman who was not only beautiful, but wise as well. From that time on he loved her even more, and they lived together happily forever after. And always, in his free moments, the King would weave his mats, so as not to forget the trade which had saved his life.

THE LITTLE GIRL LAY ON THE HEAD OF THE BEAR-SKIN RUG with her eyes half-closed like a sleepy kitten. Once more, she wanted Willie to go on reading, but Willie insisted on his right just to lie back and listen too.

The little girl laughed. "Oh, all right, if you don't want to read, then listen!"

And then she put her finger to her lips, so that he would be silent. And at that signal, a still, quiet voice came out of the chimney, and the Wind began to speak. And this is the story she told.

JOSÉ AND THE PRINCESS FLORABELLA

Once upon a time, long ago, in the land of Spain there lived a father who had two sons. The older son, whose name was José, was taken into the army and he spent long years far across the Ocean in America. While he was away, his father died, and when José returned, he found that his younger brother Juan had taken over all their father's property and belongings. He had become a rich man, whereas José had nothing more than his old army cap and a few pieces of gold from his pay in his rucksack. When he finally arrived at the family home, his younger brother Juan appeared not to recognize him. They met just at the gate, and Juan began shouting at him as if he were a beggar.

"On your way, soldier. We have nothing here for you!"

But José was not to be put off. "You mean you don't know me, Juan?" he asked.

"How should I know you?" retorted Juan. "Do you think I know every vagabond who comes this way?"

Then José revealed who he was. "I'm no vagabond, Juan", he said "I'm your older brother, José, and I've come for my share of our birthright."

This pleased Juan even less. Rudely he replied, "Father left you nothing except an old wooden chest over there in the corn-loft. He said that would be quite enough for you because you would bring home plenty of gold from America. Take it and then begone!"

José saw that he would have no luck with his brother, and so he went to the corn-loft for his inheritance. There in the corner, all by itself, stood a very, very old chest. José's first thought was to leave it there.

"What good will a battered old chest like that be to me?" he said to himself, "unless to use for firewood if I am cold."

And so good José took the chest, put it on his back, and carried it to a neighbouring house, where he rented a room. Towards evening, when the sun was setting and the wind was rising, he took an axe and began to chop the chest up for firewood. He split one board, and then another, when all at once he stopped in surprise. For as he was chopping away at the chest, a secret drawer in the bottom had suddenly come open, and out of the

56

drawer fell a piece of paper. José picked it up, looked at it, and could scarcely believe his eyes. It was a promissory note for a great deal of money which someone had owed his father.

"So Father didn't forget me after all," said José happily, and first thing next day he went to recover the money. The debtor was an honest man, and repaid the whole sum to José, right down to the last peso.

And so the veteran soldier became a rich man overnight. He no longer had to go about with his old soldier's cap on his head and an empty rucksack over his shoulder. He bought a nice house in the neighbouring town, and got himself fine new clothes and a good horse and in short, lived like a gentleman of means.

But not even all this wealth could harden his heart. One day he saw a very strange thing in the next street. Some people were shouting and dragging a dead man along the road by his legs. The dead man's wife and three children were running along behind them weeping and sobbing. José had to do something. "What is the meaning of this?" he shouted. "Can't you leave the dead in peace? What did he do to you?"

But the people turned on him angrily. "Well you may ask what he did to us! He borrowed money from us and then instead of paying it back, he died. Until his widow repays every peso, we shall not give her dead husband to her. It is our right! It is the law!"

But the poor widow had nothing. Even the roof over her head no longer belonged to her, for she had spent all her money on expensive medicines for her husband during his long illness. All she had left were three small children and eyes to cry with.

José took pity on her. "Very well," he told the people. "I shall pay the dead man's debts myself."

And so good José repaid everything the dead man owed, arranged a decent funeral for him, and gave the widow a purse of ducats for her and the children to live on. But when afterwards he counted his money, he found to his dismay that only one ducat remained from his father's inheritance.

"What now?" said José to himself, turning the single ducat over in his hand. "I won't last long with this. It will be best to look about for some employment."

And so he set his old soldier's cap on his head, threw the empty rucksack over his shoulders and set off for the royal town.

"That is the best place to look for employment," he said, and he was right. For it so happened that just then, they needed someone to look after the King's horses, and so they took on José. He worked well, and it wasn't long before he came to the attention of the King himself and soon afterwards, the King made him one of his counsellors.

While José was going up in the world, his brother Juan fell upon hard times. As long as he was well-off, he had ignored his brother, but now that he was in difficult straits, he remembered him. When he learned of José's good fortune in the King's court, he went to him for help. And José did help. He put a good word for his brother to the King and Juan received a place in the King's service.

It was a good place, but not good enough for Juan. It seemed to him that José was better off than he, and he envied him the King's favour. So he made up his mind to get rid of his brother. He kept silent about his evil intentions, however, and waited for the right time. It came when he learned that the King had once been in love with the Princess Florabella, but because he was old and ugly, the Princess had refused to marry him and hidden herself away in a castle in the middle of a deep forest. But no one knew where the castle or the forest lay.

Not even Juan knew where they were, but nevertheless one day he began to speak about the castle before the King himself. Good José happened to be somewhere else at the moment and so Juan screwed up his courage and spoke.

"Where the castle of Princess Florabella is, your majesty, I cannot say, but I do know who can show you the way there," he said.

The King's brow furrowed. "And who is it?" he asked.

"Your best counsellor, your majesty," he said. "My brother José. Several times he has boasted to me that he was there once before he entered your sevice."

The King sent for José immediately. "I hear that you know where the castle of Princess Florabella is," he roared as soon as José appeared in the doorway.

José was astonished. "How could I know that, my lord," he said, "when not even you know where it is? I have heard of this castle only from you!"

But the King did not believe him. "You lie!" he shouted. "I know that you have been there yourself, and that you have even boasted about it. Either you go there without delay and bring the Princess Florabella to me, or you shall be shorter by a head!"

José could hardly believe his ears, but when he looked at his brother and saw Juan laughing in his face, he knew at once what had happened. Bowing deeply to the King, he said, "If it be your majesty's will, then I shall set out first thing tomorrow to fetch the Princess Florabella."

And then he went sadly to the royal stables to pick a horse for the journey. But which road he should take, or where he should begin to look for the Princess Florabella, he had not the slightest idea. As he was looking over the horses and thinking about this, he suddenly noticed an old white horse in the corner. José knew all the royal mounts, but he had never seen this one before. He went over to him, and was running his hand over the horse's back when suddenly, the horse gave a merry little whinney and began to speak in a human voice. "I know what troubles you, José, but have no fear. Choose me for the journey and you will reach your destination, you will see."

José was amazed, for he had never yet heard a horse speaking the language of humans. He took the horse by the bridle, led him into the courtyard, and there he brushed him down well, gave him plenty to eat and drink, and then saddled him. And then he noticed that what had once been an old, feeble horse was now a fiery steed. When José mounted him, the white horse neighed and said, "Now we can leave, my lord, but before we start, take three loaves of bread with you for the journey. We shall need them."

José did as he was told, and put the three loaves of bread into his sack. Then they set off. As they were leaving, he saw his brother Juan smiling maliciously at him from a castle window. Now he was the King's first counsellor!

While Juan was enjoying himself in the King's court, José was making his way wearily through the wide world. The very first day, he saw a huge ant-hill by the side of the road. The white horse stopped beside it, whinneyed and said, "Those ants need your help, my lord! Throw them the three loaves of bread so that they have something to eat."

"And what shall we eat then?" said José in surprise.

But the white horse only whinneyed and said, "We shall manage, but these ants are starving and without our help, they will all die. Just do as I say and you won't regret it."

José did as he was told and threw the three loaves of bread to the ants. Then they continued on their way.

The second day they saw a hunter's net by the road and a large eagle was trapped inside, flapping its wings. The white horse stopped and said, "That eagle needs your help, my lord. Cut open the net and free it so that it can fly where it wishes."

"But what will the hunter say?" asked José in surprise.

But the white horse only whinneyed and replied, "The hunter can get along without it, but that eagle will die in captivity. Just do as I say and you won't regret it."

José obeyed this time as well and cut open the net, setting the eagle free. Then they continued on their way.

The third day they saw a fish flopping about in the sand on a river-bank. The white horse stopped and said, "That fish needs your help, my lord! Throw it back into the water so that it can swim where it wishes!"

Again José was surprised. "But what will the fisherman who threw him there say?" he asked.

But the white horse only whinneyed and said, "The fisherman can get along without it, but the fish will die on dry land. Just do as I say and you won't regret it."

And so for the third time, José obeyed the white horse. He took the fish and threw it back into the river. Then they continued on their way.

On the fourth day they entered a deep forest and in the middle of that forest they came upon a castle. It shone with a pure silver light like the full moon. But all at once that white glow dimmed and everything around began to shine as though the sun itself was coming up. But it wasn't the sun, it was the Princess Florabella. She came out of the castle with a basket of golden wheat and began to throw it to the chickens. There were as many of them as there were stars in the heavens.

And the white horse whinneyed quietly and said, "Listen carefully, my lord. I will take you up to the castle, and there I will trot and dance about so prettily that the Princess will not be able to resist asking you to let her ride me. This you will allow her to do. But as soon as she is in the saddle, I shall begin to rear and buck and the Princess will be afraid. Then you will tell her that I am not used to having a woman in the saddle, and you will jump up behind her. Once you are in the saddle, the Princess will be ours. I shall take off at a gallop with you both and I won't stop until we are back at the castle of our King."

Everything happened as the good white horse said it would. Suspecting nothing, the Princess mounted the horse excitedly and prepared to ride, but the horse would not take a step. It bucked and reared, and it would not obey until José swung into the saddle. It galloped off with both of them and ran through the deep forest, ignoring the roads

When the Princess finally realized that she was being carried off, she dropped the basket she was carrying and the grain in it flew out in all directions.

"Stop," she begged José, "and wait while I gather up the grain."

But José would not stop and wait. "There is grain enough where we are going," he said.

Just then they rode under a spreading oak tree and the Princess lifted up her shawl so that it caught in the branches and hung there.

"Stop," she pleaded, "and wait while I go back for my shawl."

But José would not stop and wait. "There are shawls enough where we are going," was all he said.

Just then they rode across a river and the Princess took her ring off her finger and let it drop into the water.

"Stop for just a moment," she implored, "and wait while I find my ring."

But even then José would not stop and wait. "There are rings enough where we are going," he replied, and on they rode.

And before long they were back at the King's castle. The old King was beside himself with joy to see his beloved Florabella again, and he once more smiled favourably on José. But Juan was even more sullen then before.

The King's favour and Juan's sulleness, however, did not last for long, for the Princess Florabella refused even to see the old King. She locked herself in her chambers with seven locks, and admitted no one, not even the King himself. When he knocked on her door and pleaded with her to open, the Princess snapped back, "I shall not open the door until you bring me everything I lost on the way."

And the King frowned deeply and sent for José. "You brought me Princess Florabella, and now you must bring me everything which she lost on the way!" he stormed. "Only you know what she lost and where she lost it. If you do not bring me everything within three days, you shall be shorter by a head!"

The old King scowled fiercely, while brother Juan merely laughed. Poor José bowed deeply before the King and said, "If it be your majesty's will, I shall set out first thing tomorrow."

And then he went sadly to the stable to his white horse. But the horse welcomed him with a merry neigh and said, "I know what troubles you, my lord, but there is nothing to fear. Jump into the saddle and you will see, everything will be all right again."

And so José set out into the world a second time. As he was leaving, his brother Juan leered maliciously from the castle window.

While Juan was enjoying himself in the King's court, José was making his way wearily through the wide world. The first day he came to the river where the Princess Florabella had lost her ring. But how was he to find it in such deep water? Poor José searched all around but in vain, for the water had long ago swallowed up the ring. "I'll never find it," he sighed sadly, "not even if I look for ever."

But the white horse merely whinneyed and said, "Ah, but you will, my lord! Just ask that fish you once helped."

And so José did what the horse had told him. He called out to the fish, and lo and

behold, the fish really did appear. It stuck its head out of the water and said, "What do you want, José? Just tell me, and I shall help you with pleasure."

"I need Princess Florabella's ring," he said. "She dropped it into this river when we were crossing it."

"Nothing easier!" said the fish, and with a flip of its tail it was gone. In a little while, it was back with the Princess's ring in its mouth.

"Here it is, José," it said. "I hope it brings you good luck."

José thanked the fish with all his heart, swung into the saddle, and off they went. The second day they came to the deep forest where the Princess Florabella had lost her shawl. But how was he to find it in such a vast wood? Poor José looked around in vain, for the forest had long ago swallowed up the shawl. "I'll never find it," he sighed sadly, "not even if I look forever."

But the white horse merely neighed and said, "Ah, but you will, my lord! Just ask that eagle you once helped."

And so José did what the horse had told him. He called out to the eagle, and lo and behold, the eagle really did appear. It flew down from the clouds and said, "What do you want, José? Just tell me and I shall be glad to help you."

"I must find Princess Florabella's shawl," said José. "She lost it in this deep forest as we were riding through it."

"Nothing easier!" said the eagle, and it spread its wings, flew over the thick forest and in a little while, it was back with the Princess's shawl in its beak.

"Here it is, José," said the eagle. "May it bring you good luck!"

José thanked the eagle with all his heart, swung into the saddle, and urged the white horse on. The third day they came to the forest where the Princess had dropped her basket of golden wheat. José found the basket without much difficulty, but how was he to gather up the grain in the dense undergrowth? Poor José looked around in vain, for the forest had long since swallowed up the golden wheat.

"I'll never be able to find it all," he sighed sadly, "not even if I keep looking till the end of my days."

But the white horse just neighed and said, "Ah, but you will, my lord! Just ask the ants you once helped."

And so José did what the horse had said. He called out to the ants, and lo and behold, the ants really did appear suddenly out of the grass and they said. "What do you want, José? Just tell us, and we shall be glad to help."

"I need to gather up the golden grain which belongs to Princess Florabella. She scattered it in these woods when we were passing through."

"Nothing easier!" said the ants, and they ran off into the dark forest. In a little while they were back, bringing with them every last grain of wheat.

"Here it is, José," they said. "May it bring you luck and a beautiful wife."

José thanked the ants from the bottom of his heart. He swung into the saddle, urged his horse for home, and before they knew it, the royal castle was looming up ahead. The old King was overjoyed that José had brought what his beloved Princess had wanted, and he smiled favourably on José. But Juan was even more sullen than before.

Once more, however, neither the King's favour nor brother Juan's sullenness lasted for long, for the Princess still did not open her door to the old King, not even when he brought her the wheat, the shawl and the ring. When he knocked on her door, and pleaded with her to open it, the Princess snapped, "I won't open the door until you throw that brigand who deprived me of all my treasure into boiling oil."

And once more the King frowned and roared at José, "Since you brought me the Princess Florabella, you must jump into a kettle of boiling oil for her. If you don't do it yourself, I shall have you thrown in."

While the old King frowned, José's brother Juan merely laughed. Poor José bowed deeply before the King and said, "If it is your majesty's will, I shall jump into the boiling oil myself. Only grant me one last wish, that I may say farewell to my faithful white horse."

And then he went sadly to see his horse. But the horse greeted him as usual with a cheerful whinney and said. "I know what troubles you, my lord! But there is nothing to fear. Jump into my saddle and ride me around as fast as you can until I am covered in sweat. Then rub yourself all over with my sweat and you will see that the boiling oil will not harm you."

José did as the white horse had said. He jumped into the saddle, and rode him as fast as he could around the castle courtyard, then rubbed himself from head to toe with the horse's sweat.

In the meantime, they had heated a huge kettle of oil over a fire in the courtyard. José stepped up to it apprehensively, and then jumped in. Lo and behold, the boiling oil did not harm him, and when he jumped out again, he was hale and hearty and a hundred times more dashing than before. Everyone was astounded, but no one more than the Princess Florabella. She had seen everything through her window and she fell in love with José at once.

When the King saw what had happened to José and how the boiling oil had made him even more handsome he decided to try it too. He went up to the kettle, and without another thought, jumped in. But it didn't turn out as he had expected. Before he could cry for help, he was gone, and only his golden crown was left floating on the surface.

No one was very sorry, no one wept for the old King, but José's brother Juan trembled with fear. And he trembled even more when all the people assembled before the royal castle and named good José as their king. Juan gathered up what he could and ran away somewhere into the wide world.

And while Juan was making his way wearily through the wide world, José was enjoying himself in the royal castle. And why shouldn't he, since he was getting ready to marry the Princess Florabella! And when they married, it was a wedding the like of which the world had never seen. José was indebted for all his good fortune and all that glory to his faithful white horse.

Good José knew this and went to the stable to thank his horse from the bottom of his heart. The white horse greeted him as usual with a merry neigh, but then he said, "Do not thank me, my lord. I have merely repaid an old favour. Do you remember that poor man whose debts you paid and whom you gave a decent burial? I am that poor man.

I have served you until I was able to help you to good fortune. But now you no longer need me, and so, good luck and remember that good deeds always bear fruit."

And before good José could say anything in reply, the white horse was gone, vanished like a wisp of fog that the wind blows away. But the young King remembered him as long as he lived, and whenever he could, he told his children and his grandchildren how the faithful white horse, in his gratitude, had helped him to gain the throne and the Princess Florabella.

ALL DAY WILLIE WAS AWFULLY TEMPTED to ask Granny about the little girl from the fireplace, but he finally decided not to. Perhaps Granny wouldn't believe him. And anyway, she would certainly know that he didn't go right to bed at night and she would make him sleep with her in the kitchen. So instead, he only asked her to let him have some more books to read.

Granny shook her head. "You don't mean you want to read them, Willie?" she asked. She knew very well that Willie was not much of a reader, for he always used to complain and say that he was too small. The truth was that he preferred having Granny read to him.

In fact, he was just like the little girl from the fireplace. Almost before Granny had closed the door behind her, there she was, sitting on the bear-skin rug, asking for a fairy-tale.

"Don't speak so loudly," said Willie in alarm, "Granny will hear you!"

But the little girl only laughed and said, "Don't worry, she won't hear me!"

And that evening, they didn't play hide-and-seek or tag. Willie had already chosen a story, and all he had to do was open the book at the place and begin to read. And this is what he read.

PUSS-IN-BOOTS
AND THE BIRD KING

Once upon a time there was a poor collier who lived in a cottage in the middle of the woods with his wife and his baby boy. Soon after the child was born the collier and his wife died, leaving the poor little fellow, who was still in nappies, all alone and completely helpless. He would have died too, of course, if the sound of his crying hadn't caught the ears of a puss who was wandering through the woods. He was a beautiful puss, with two round green glowing eyes and a coat of fur that glittered like pure gold.

The puss looked after the poor orphan child. He fed him, changed his nappies, taught him to walk and even to speak. The little boy knew no one else except Puss, and he loved him as though he were his own mother and father.

The puss did everything he could for the orphan. He even made clothes for him when the boy began to grow up. He fashioned him trousers and a jacket from animal skins and he wove him a cloak from the most beautiful feathers he could find. And truly, there was not a king alive who had such a magnificent garment.

"You look like the King of all the birds in your cloak", said Puss proudly when the boy threw it over his shoulders "And now that you have such a royal cloak, I shall get a royal crown for you as well. You shall marry the daughter of our King!"

The boy was startled at this. "What are you talking about, Puss?" he said. "How could a poor fellow like me ever marry the Princess? Why I have nothing at all in which to appear before her."

But Puss was not to be put off. "Don't worry, my boy," he said. "Just do as I say. First, bring me your father's old boots from the cupboard, so that I can take the King a gift."

The collier's son didn't know what to make of all this, but he brought the boots, gave them a good polish, and helped Puss put them on. When Puss walked around in them, and when he set the collier's wide-brimmed hat on his head, he looked for all the world like a real knight.

With no futher ado, Puss set out for the royal castle in his high boots. His golden fur shone so brilliantly that all the rabbits ran from the fields and gathered round him. "Hello there, Sir Puss, tell us where you got such a fine golden coat and those beautiful boots and hat?" they called.

"That is a secret," replied Puss cleverly. "But if you wish come with me and you can each have a coat like mine."

The rabbits believed him and ran after Puss until they came to the King's castle. When the gate had closed behind them, Puss-in-Boots called out boldly. "Your Majesty! Come out and receive greetings from my Master the Bird King. He sends you a gift of some of his finest game."

The King could hardly believe his eyes when he stepped through the door. The whole court-yard was full of sleek fat rabbits.

"He must be a very rich King," he said to himself, "but it is strange that I have never heard of him."

And then he graciously invited Puss-in-Boots in, feasted him royally, and as Puss was leaving, thanked him and said, "Give my greetings to your master, Sir Puss, and tell him that I would be delighted to meet him."

The next time Puss-in-Boots came to visit the King, he brought him a whole court-yard full of foxes, and the third time, a whole court-yard full of bears. The King was overwhelmed. "This Bird King must truly be a wealthy man," he said to himself. "He would make a fine bridegroom for my daughter."

And when Puss was taking leave of the King for the third time, the King said to him graciously, "Give my greetings to your master, Sir Puss, and tell him that I shall expect a visit from him tomorrow."

Puss ran merrily home. "Get ready, my lad," he said. "Tomorrow we are going to see the King!"

But the collier's son was alarmed. "There you go again, Puss," he said. "How can I ever appear before the King in these ragged skins of mine?"

But Puss was not to be put off. "Don't worry about a thing," he said. "Haven't I told you just to do as I say? Now, on the way to the King's castle there is a pond. When we go by it, I want you to throw off your skins and jump into the water. Leave the rest to me. "

The collier's son didn't know what to make of all this, but he did as Puss said. Early next morning they set off for the royal castle. Puss strode along in his boots and wide-brimmed hat and the collier's son followed behind in his clothes of skin and his cloak of feathers. When they came to the pond, the lad threw off his cape and skins and jumped into the water.

Puss-in-Boots hid the skins under some bushes, and left the cape of feathers on the bank, and then at the top of his voice he began to shout. "Help, robbers, help! Come who may!"

When they heard his cry, the King's guard came running from the castle and soon afterwards the King himself arrived with his advisors and courtiers.

"What ever is going on, Sir Puss?" asked the King.

"We were on our way to visit you, your majesty," said Puss, "but right here beneath your very castle, robbers fell upon us and took everything we have. They took all the clothes off my master, the Bird King, and threw him into the water. I was able to save only his cloak. Just look!"

The King looked at the collier boy's cloak of feathers and he could scarcely believe his eyes, for not even he possessed such a magnificent garment.

"This Bird King must be a rich man indeed," he said to himself, "if he travels in something so magnificent."

And he immediately ordered his advisors and courtiers to take the Bird King to the best chambers in the castle and there to fit him out with the finest clothing in the royal wardrobe.

The collier's son was not sure whether he was awake or dreaming. The King's advisors and courtiers led him to the King's best chambers and there they dressed him in the

68

King's finest apparel, and when he appeared before the King and the Princess, both of them just sat and looked at him, for they had never seen such a dashing young man in their lives.

The King and his daughter couldn't take their eyes off the Bird King, and the Bird King, for his part, could scarcely stop staring at all the wondrous things he saw around him. And the most marvellous of all was the Princess herself. Never in his life had he seen anyone as beautiful as she. At first, her beauty was such that he could scarcely find his tongue. But he soon became bolder and in a few days, he was already believing that he really was the Bird King and that he really did have a royal castle instead of just an old tumble-down cottage in the middle of the woods. When a month had gone by, however, the old King called the lad back to his senses. He was curious about the Bird kingdom, and when the Bird King failed to invite him for a visit the old King simply invited himself.

"We thank you for your visit, good sir," he said, "and if you have no objections, we shall return you the favour tomorrow and come to visit you."

The collier's son was alarmed. What should he do now? He simply couldn't take the King to his dilapidated cottage in the woods. But Puss was alert and answered in his place.

"You shall be welcome, your majesty, but permit me to travel ahead of you to show the way."

The next day the King set out with a huge retinue. He sat in a golden coach with his daughter and the Bird King and behind them came a procession of other carriages and horsemen. But Puss-in-Boots hurried on ahead. Before long he saw a huge flock of sheep by the road accompanied by three shepherds.

"Hey there, shepherds," he called out to them, "to whom do those sheep belong?"

"To our master, Sir Puss," they replied respectfully, "a powerful ogre who lives in a castle beyond those woods."

Puss-in-Boots shook his head. "I wouldn't say that if I were you, shepherds, not if you value your lives. For just behind me, the Bird King is coming with a huge procession and if he heard what you've just said, he would have your heads cut off. You had better say that they belong to him, and then half of this flock will be yours!"

The shepherds were delighted. "Long live the Bird King! Long live the Bird King!" they shouted.

And it wasn't long before the royal procession arrived. The King looked out of his coach and asked the shepherds whom the sheep belonged to. As one man, they cried out gaily, "To whom else but our lord and master the Bird King!"

And just as Puss-in-Boots had persuaded the shepherds, so further on the road he persuaded some cowherds, and still further on, some men who were looking after a herd of horses. And every time the King would ask them to whom these herds belonged, the men would cry out merrily as one man, "To whom else but our lord and master the Bird King!"

The King was amazed, for not even he had so many sheep, cows and horses. And he was even more amazed when an enormous castle loomed up ahead of them.

In that castle lived the powerful man-eating ogre. Puss-in-Boots had long known about him and now he fearlessly pounded on the gate and cried, "Hey there, let me in, good people, you have a visitor."

The man-eating ogre was always glad of guests, especially if he could have them for supper. He came himself to open the door, but when he saw Puss-in-Boots standing on the threshold, he was quite taken aback, for he had never had such a guest before. All the same, he invited him in politely.

"Welcome, Sir Puss, and tell me what brings you here to me?"

Now the ogre was truly terrifying. He was as tall as a tree, with a head as big as a barrel, eyes like soup-bowls, and teeth like a saw. But Puss-in-Boots was not afraid.

"I have heard of your magic powers, good sir," he said. "They say you can change yourself into any animal you wish. Is it true?"

The man-eating ogre laughed boastfully and said, "Why of course it is! Just watch closely, and don't be afraid."

And in that very instant a huge lion stood where the ogre had been a moment before. The lion roared so loudly that Puss was truly frightened and he jumped behind the door in a flash. But when he peeped out again, there was only the ogre standing in the doorway, and he laughed and laughed.

Puss-in-Boots recovered quickly from his fright. "I see, good sir," he said, "that you are truly a great magician. You can certainly change yourself into a lion. But could you change yourself even into a tiny mouse?"

The man-eating ogre laughed boastfully and replied, "And why not? Just watch closely, but don't be startled." And in a trice, a little mouse crouched squeaking in the doorway where the giant had stood. But this time, Puss-in-Boots was not frightened in the least. He jumped on the mouse and gobbled it up, skin and bones and all. And just then, the King's golden coach drove up with the King himself, the Princess, and the collier's son inside.

Puss-in-Boots welcomed them in the doorway. "Please come in, your majesty. Please come in, your highness. The castle of the Bird King is ready and waiting for you."

Now the old King had a beautiful castle, but the giant's castle was a hundred times more magnificent, and more than that, it was a magic castle. Invisible hands opened doors for them, invisible hands laid the table for their banquet, invisible hands brought the guests their food and drink, as much as their hearts desired. Neither the Princess nor the King himself had ever seen anything so splendid before.

And now the King no longer hesitated. "I see, O Bird King, that you are a hundred times richer than I. You have everything you could want except a wife. If you wish, I shall give you the hand of my beloved daughter in marriage."

The collier's son did not know whether he was awake or sleeping. He could scarcely speak for joy, but then he found his tongue and said, "Thank you, your majesty, and thank you, beautiful Princess. If you will be mine, I shall truly no longer want for anything."

And so Puss-in-Boots began to prepare the wedding. It was a splendid wedding, more magnificent than even the King himself had had when he married the Queen. A thou-

sand guests from every corner of the world were invited, but the most respected guest of all of course, was, Puss-in-Boots. He sat in the place of honour right next to the Bird King, and no one could take their eyes off him, for the guests had never seen such a handsome best man before, with such a magnificent golden fur coat and such a splendid wide-brimmed hat.

And when at last the wedding was over and the guests had gone home, leaving the Bird King and his bride alone in their happiness, Puss-in-Boots lived on with them and was their closest friend and wisest counsellor for ever after. At least, so it is told in the story of Puss-in-Boots and the Bird King.

*THE LITTLE GIRL LIKED WILLIE'S FAIRY-
TALES.* "They're very nice," she said. "I don't know any like
them."

Willie was happy to hear her say this. "They're stories my
Granny tells me," he said proudly. "But yours are very beautiful too, and quite different."

The little girl was pleased. "They're my mother's stories," she
said. Would you like to hear another one?"

Willie nodded eagerly. And the little girl put her finger to
her lips, indicating that she wanted him to be silent and listen.
And then the still, quiet voice of the Wind sounded in the
chimney and began to speak. And this is the tale she told.

YOUTH WITHOUT AGE
AND LIFE WITHOUT DEATH

Once upon a time, very long ago, there lived a powerful King and his Queen. They were both young: he was dashing and she was beautiful, and they were very happy together. Both of them wanted very much to have a child, but as the years went by and no child came, the King and Queen began to be troubled. They sought the advice of physicians, they consulted astrologers, and when none of this helped, they began to go to herb doctors and wizards. Finally, they learned of a wise old man who lived in a certain village far away. The King and Queen sent messengers requesting him to come to the royal court and advise them, but the old man refused. "The King has just as far to come to me as I have to go to him," he told the King's messengers. "If he needs something from me, let him come here; he will be welcome. But I am an old man and in my old age, I shall go nowhere."

And so the King and Queen had to go to visit the old man.

They travelled in great pomp, accompanied by the entire royal court and a full complement of the royal guard. When they arrived at the edge of the village, the old man was waiting for them.

"Welcome, oh King. Welcome, beautiful Queen!" he said. "I know what you want of me, but I am afraid I can offer you little consolation, for what you desire will bring you more cares than pleasures. In the end, you may even regret it."

"We shall not regret it," said the King confidently. "Just tell us whether you can give us some herbs so that we may have children."

"I can," said the old man. "Here they are. If the Queen boils them and drinks the potion from them, she will have a child in a year and a day. He shall be called Valiant, but he shall not be a joy and a comfort to you for long. Thus it is written!"

"We shall see about that," said the King. He took the magic herbs from the old man and returned to the royal castle with his wife and their procession.

The old man's herbs were truly magic. In a year and a day, the Queen gave birth to a son, a little boy with hair like the sun and eyes like stars. But alas, no sooner had the boy been born than his beautiful eyes filled with tears, and he began to cry without ceasing. They tried everything. They rocked him in his cradle, dandled him on their knees, held him in their arms. They even tried different medicines. But nothing helped. The little Prince lay in his cradle and cried and cried until his parents thought their hearts would break.

When his father the King heard about it, he sat down beside the cradle and tried to cheer his little son up, saying "Don't cry, my child. Don't weep, my son. When you grow up, I shall give you my royal crown and sceptre and you will be the most powerful King in the world!"

But the little Prince kept on crying. And his father the King tried again, saying, "Don't cry, my child, don't weep, my son. When you grow up I shall give you the most beautiful Princess in the world as your wife!"

But even this did not stop the little Prince's tears. And so his father tried a third time.

"Don't cry, my child," he said soothingly, "Do not weep, my son. When you grow up, I shall give you youth without age and life without death."

The King did not know why he had said this but no sooner had the words left his lips than the Prince suddenly stopped crying and smiled like the sun coming out from behind the clouds.

From that time on, the Prince never cried again. Each day he grew taller and taller like spring grain, and each day he became more and more stalwart and handsome: well he deserved the name Valiant. And just as he was stalwart and handsome, so he was clever and quick-witted and it wasn't long before even the best tutors in the land had taught him all they knew.

Their son was a constant source of joy to his mother and father and they had long forgotten what the wise old man from the village had told them. But one day the good Prince himself reminded them of it. It was on the very day he turned fifteen and the whole court was sitting round the banquet table, when suddenly Valiant stood up and said, "Dear Father, the time has come for you to keep your word and give me what you promised."

The King was surprised. "And what is that, my son? Tell me and it shall be yours."

And Valiant replied. "Father, I want you to give me youth without age and life without death."

And then the King remembered the promise he had given to his son as a baby. He lowered his head and said, "How can I give it to you, my son, when I don't possess it myself, nor even know whether such a thing exists in this world. I do not know why I promised it to you then, but you were weeping so sorrowfully that I didn't quite know what I was saying."

And now Prince Valiant lowered his head and said, "If you cannot give it to me, Father, then I must go and search for it myself. Otherwise I perish of grief here even sooner than I would have in the cradle."

In vain did the King and Queen plead with him not to go, in vain did the counsellors and lords of the court urge him to stay and help his mother and father rule. Prince Valiant would not be persuaded. And finally everyone became reconciled to the idea, and his father and mother gave him their royal blessing for the long journey ahead.

And so Prince Valiant made ready to go into the world. First of all he went to the royal stables to choose a good horse. There were more than enough of them there, each one finer than the one before, but none was good enough for Prince Valiant. For as soon as he placed his hand on any horse's back, the animal would whinny and drop to its knees under the weight. The Prince went through the whole stable and still he could not find a horse to suit him. At last, in the corner, he saw a horse he had missed before, an old nag covered with scars and welts, a bundle of skin and bones. The horse raised his head to look at him and the Prince said to himself, "Well, since I've tried so many I'll try this one too."

And when he stepped up to the horse and placed his hand on its back, a strange thing happened. The old horse neighed happily. He didn't move nor did he drop to his knees. "This is the horse for me," said Prince Valiant.

And the old horse answered him in a human voice, "What is it you wish, my Lord? I am glad to feel the hand of a real warrior on my back once more!"

And Prince Valiant replied, "I'm going into the world, old fellow, I am going to look for youth without age and life without death."

"Then we have a long journey ahead of us, my Lord!" said the horse. "But if you will put your trust in me, I shall take you there. But first you must brush me for six weeks and feed me oatmeal boiled in milk for six weeks and then I shall be ready for the journey. And you too, Prince Valiant, you must make ready. Ask your father the King for the weapons he had when he was young. Ask him to give you his sword, his spear and his bow and arrows. You won't be sorry you have them, believe me!"

Prince Valiant did as the old horse had told him, and it was well he did so. For six weeks he brushed the horse with his own hands, six weeks he fed him oatmeal boiled in milk, and when the six weeks were over, he laid his hand on him, and the old horse shook himself. As soon as he did so, his scarred old hide fell away from him like a snake-skin and before Prince Valiant stood a handsome, powerful steed with wings on his shoulders. And in a human voice the horse said, "Now I am at your service, my Lord, and we can set off if you are ready."

Valiant was also prepared. He asked his father the King for the weapons he had used when he was young, and with a sigh, the King agreed. "Go and find them, my son, they are yours," he said. "They will be in one of the chests in our treasury, but I don't know myself where they are. It has been such a long time since I have worn my sword, spear, bow and arrows."

The Prince looked through all the chests in the royal treasury, and there were more than enough of them there, each one more beautiful than the one before. But in none of them could he find what he was looking for. Finally, in one corner of the treasury, he saw the last chest, a very old and battered one. Valiant went over to it and said to himself, "Well, since I've already opened so many, I'll open this one too."

And then he lifted the lid and it was well he did so! For in the chest lay his father's sword, spear and bow and arrows, but all so old and rusty and covered with dust that they would have discouraged anyone.

Prince Valiant however was not to be disheartened, and for six weeks he cleaned the weapons, six weeks he repaired them, and when on the seventh week, he buckled on his father's sword, grasped his lance and slung the bow and quiver of arrows over his shoulder, he felt a hundred times more powerful than before.

"And now I have everything I need," he said joyfully. "Tomorrow we shall set out!"

The next day a great sorrow fell upon the royal palace, for Prince Valiant was taking leave of his parents.

"Farewell Father, farewell Mother," he said. "I thank you for everything you have done for me."

"Farewell, my son, I pray you will come back safely and soon," said the Queen in tears.

"Farewell, lad," said the King with a sigh, "and remember, we are old now and cannot wait for long."

But Prince Valiant had already swung onto his horse and was urging it through the castle gate, followed by his retinue, a hundred horsemen on good mounts and a hundred wagons with provisions and gifts to last a whole year.

As soon as they had crossed the borders of his father's kingdom, however, Prince Valiant stopped his horse, turned to his men and said, "Thank you all for accompanying me, friends, but I shall not need you any longer. Divide up everything in the wagons equally among yourselves, and return home. I shall continue on alone."

And so Prince Valiant and his retainers parted. The Prince went straight on, road or no road, towards the rising sun and his retainers returned the way they had come, towards the setting sun. After three days and three nights Valiant came to a wide, flat desert set about with human bones. Beyond the flat land a dense black forest loomed and when the Prince stopped at its edge, the winged horse spoke to him and said, "Beware, my Lord. We have come to the borders of the Owl Crone's domain. She was once the daughter of a certain powerful King, but so evil and arrogant was she that her parents cursed her, and she changed into a huge bloodthirsty bird. She will mercilessly slay anyone who sets foot inside her domain, but you need not be afraid. Prepare your bow and arrows so they will be at hand when you need them."

"Prepare them I shall," said the Prince, and slipped his bow from his shoulder. Then they lay down to rest. Prince Valiant stood watch until midnight, and then his faithful winged horse stood watch until morning. As soon as day broke, the horse awoke his

master. "Arise, Valiant, the sun is coming up and we have a hard journey ahead of us through the woods of the Owl Crone."

Prince Valiant jumped to his feet, saddled his faithful horse, and then mounted him, bow in hand. At that very instant a frightful clamour arose from the woods, as though someone was breaking down the trees.

"Beware, my Lord," said the horse in a human voice. "That is the Owl Crone, and she's making straight for us."

And sure enough, an old hag as big as a mountain and as ugly as night was crashing through the woods. She had a human body and the head of a bird with a huge beak, and she broke the trees around her as she went like matchsticks. It was a terryfying sight.

The horse did not wait for the Owl Crone to reach them. He spread his wings, and rose into the air like the wind. Prince Valiant drew an arrow from his quiver, set it to the string, drew back the bow, and let it loose. The arrow whistled through the air and struck off the Owl Crone's leg. She cried out in pain, saying, "Cease your shooting, Prince Valiant. I see you are the stronger. But without your faithful horse you would be helpless and I would have eaten you just like all the others who have dared to step inside my domain. But now you have nothing to fear. You are my guest!"

Prince Valiant leaned over and whispered into the winged horse's ear, "What do you think, my faithful steed? Can I believe her?"

And in a human voice the horse replied, "You can, my Lord. She will not harm you now. But take that leg of hers with you!"

Valiant stuck the old crone's leg into a sack and set out with her for her palace in the middle of the woods. And there the Owl Crone feasted him as befits a Prince. He hadn't eaten so well since leaving his father's castle. But the Owl Crone ate nothing; she just sat by the table wincing and writhing with pain. And Prince Valiant took pity on her, drew her leg from the sack, and when he placed it against her wound, the leg instantly grew back again. The Owl Crone embraced the Prince out of sheer joy and in her gratitude, she wanted to give him one of her three daughters as his wife. They were as beautiful as the morning sun, but the Prince thanked her and refused.

"I shall not marry," he said, "until I find youth without age and life without death."

"Then you will search for a long time yet," said the Owl Crone. "But with a horse like that, perhaps you will succeed. In the meantime, however, you may both rest here with me a while before travelling on."

Three days and three nights the Owl Crone entertained Prince Valiant before letting him go on. On the morning of the fourth day, the Prince jumped into the saddle and took his leave.

"Farewell, Owl Crone, farewell beautiful maidens," he said, "for I must be on my way."

"Farewell, Valiant," said the Owl Crone, "and may you find what you are looking for!" And her beautiful daughters echoed the good wish, but the Prince was already far away.

For three weeks the Prince rode straight on towards the rising sun, until finally he came to a huge meadow at the edge of a woods. Half of the meadow was set about with brightly coloured flowers and tall, green grass, and the other half lay burned and dry as though it was suffering from a terrible drought. When the Prince stopped there for a rest, the winged horse said to him, "Beware, my Lord! We have come to the borders of the Dragon Crone's domain. She is the sister of the Owl Crone, and because she was even more evil and arrogant, her parents placed a curse upon her and she changed into a two-headed dragon. But she hates her own sister, and wherever she can, she does her harm. That is why half this meadow is burned. And she will mercilessly burn anyone who dares to set foot inside her domain. But you need not be afraid. Prepare your sword so that it will be at hand when you need it."

"Prepare it I shall," said Prince Valiant, and he unsheathed his sword. Then they lay down to rest. Prince Valiant stood watch until midnight, and his faithful winged horse stood watch until morning. As soon as day broke, the horse awoke his master.

"Arise, Valiant. The sun is coming up and a difficult journey through the wood of the Dragon Crone awaits us."

Prince Valiant jumped to his feet, saddled the faithful horse and mounted him, sword in hand. Suddenly a frightful clamour arose from the woods, as though someone were knocking over the trees.

"Beware, my Lord," said the horse. "That is the Dragon Crone and she is making straight for us!"

And sure enough, an old hag bigger than a mountain and uglier than night was rushing through the woods. She had a human body and two dragon heads and as she went, she broke the trees around her like matchsticks. It was a terrifying sight.

The horse did not wait for the Dragon Crone to reach them. He spread his wings and rose into the air like the wind. Prince Valiant swung his sword and cut off one of the Dragon Crone's heads. She cried out in pain, saying, "Stop swinging your sword, Valiant. I see now that you are the stronger. But you would be helpless without your faithful horse and I would have burned you like all the others who have dared to step inside my domain. But now you have nothing to fear. You are my guest!"

Prince Valiant leaned over and whispered into the winged horse's ear, "What do you think, my faithful steed? Can I believe her?"

And in a human voice, the horse replied, "You can, my Lord. She will not harm you now. But take that head of hers with you."

Valiant stuck the old crone's head into his sack and set out with her for her palace in the middle of the woods. There the Dragon Crone feasted him as befits a prince. Not even the Owl Crone had fed him so well. But the Dragon Crone ate nothing. She just sat by the table wincing and writhing with pain. And Prince Valiant took pity on her, drew the head he had cut off from his sack and when he placed it against the open wound, the head instantly grew back again. The Dragon Crone embraced the Prince out of sheer joy and in her gratitude, she wanted to give him one of her daughters as his wife. They were more beautiful than the morning sun, but the Prince, thanking her, refused.

"I shall not marry," he said, "until I find youth without age and life without death."

"Then you will search for a long time yet," said the Dragon Crone. "But with a horse like that, perhaps you will succeed after all. In the meantime, however, you may both rest here with me before travelling on."

Three nights and three days the Dragon Crone entertained Valiant before letting him go on. On the morning of the fourth day, the Prince jumped into the saddle and took his leave.

"Farewell, Dragon Crone, farewell, beautiful maidens," he said, "for I must be going."

"Farewell, Valiant," said the Dragon Crone, "and may you find what you are looking for!" Her beautiful daughters echoed the good wish, but the Prince was already well on his way.

For three months Prince Valiant rode straight on towards the rising sun, until at last he came to a great plain full of flowers, each one more beautiful than the one before. On the other side of the plain, however, there loomed a deep and tangled forest.

When the Prince stopped before it to rest a little, the winged horse said to him, "Beware, my Lord. We have come to the borders of the land of eternal Spring. And now the greatest test of all awaits us. Beyond this plain there is a deep forest full of wild animals. Your bow, sword and spear would be useless against them, so we must fly over it. If we succeed we shall be at our destination, for in the middle of that forest is the palace of youth without age and life without death. Rest well, so that you will be ready in the morning."

"Rest I shall," said Prince Valiant, and he lay down to sleep. This time the faithful winged horse stood watch all night. Just as dawn was breaking, he awakened his master. "Arise, Valiant," he said. "The sun is coming up and we have a difficult journey yet to the palace of youth without age and life without death."

Prince Valiant jumped to his feet, saddled his faithful horse and mounted him, when suddenly, a frightful clamour arose from the forest.

"Beware, my Lord," said the horse. "Those are the wild animals from the forest. We must wait until they go to drink. Then we can try."

"Very well, old fellow," said the Prince, and they waited until the clamour from the dark forest had died down. Then the Prince spurred his horse.

"Hold tightly, my Lord," cried the horse, and he spread his wings and rose high above the forest so swiftly that Prince Valiant had to grasp his mane with both hands so that the wind would not carry him away. And then something sparkled ahead of them, and the Prince saw below a magnificent palace in the middle of a huge park. The winged horse slowly descended towards it, but alas, before he could alight in the courtyard in front of the palace, he brushed his hoof against the top of a tree and the whole forest began to resound as if a tightly stretched string had been plucked. Instantly from all sides, savage beasts began rushing up with such a frightful howling and yelping that the Prince was terrified. And there would have been trouble enough for the Prince and his faithful horse had not a maiden as beautiful as a fairy come out of the castle just at that moment to feed her little darlings, as she called those wild animals.

The maiden was amazed. As long as the castle had been standing, not a living soul had ever come to visit, and now suddenly she saw before her a handsome Prince and a horse with wings on his shoulders. She raised her hand and at once the wild beasts drew back and became as silent as a flock of sheep.

"Welcome, Prince," said the beautiful Fairy. "What do you seek here?"

"I'm seeking youth without age and life without death," answered Prince Valiant.

"Then you have come to the proper place," said the fairy and she led Prince Valiant into the palace. There her two older sisters greeted the Prince. They were just as lovely and just as kind, but the Prince liked the youngest best of all.

The three fairy sisters spread a fine feast for Prince Valiant and afterwards they prepared a bed for him. "You shall tell us everything once you have had a good sleep," they said.

And so Prince Valiant and his faithful horse rested. They slept for three days and nights before they recovered from their long and arduous journey. It wasn't until the fourth day that Prince Valiant told the beautiful maidens who he was and what he was looking for, how he had set forth into the world and everything he had experienced. The fairy sisters listened in amazement, for they had never heard anything like that before. And when the Prince had finished they asked him to stay with them forever. They had grown very fond of him and with him around, things were much gayer in that lonely place where they had lived as long as they had been alive.

"Many people desire to come to the palace of youth without age and life without death," they said, "but you are the first who has ever made the long journey here." And so the Prince remained in the palace of the beautiful fairies. The days flew by in joy and pleasure as if they were in paradise, and his joy and pleasure became even greater when, after a time, he took youngest and most beautiful sister as his wife.

"Now you belong to us," the three fairy sisters told him, "and now you can ride wherever you wish in our wide land. But there is one valley beyond the wood where you must never dare to venture. It is the Valley of Grief and whoever sets foot in it will carry grief and sorrow with him for the rest of his life."

"Why should I go there?" laughed Prince Valiant, and he quite put the valley out of his mind. And why not, when he was so happy with his wife and her sisters! He visited their golden palaces with them, walked with them through the beautiful parks, and gardens, went riding with them in the deep woods, and the days, weeks and months flew by in pure joy. And whenever he felt like riding by himself, he would go hunting.

One day while out hunting a strange thing happened to him. He was chasing after a rabbit and he shot at it with his bow, but missed, and the rabbit ran off. Valiant urged on his horse, shot once more, but again he missed. In his zeal, he paid little heed to where he was going, urged his horse on for the third time, and shot again. This time his arrow found its mark, but when he jumped down from his horse to pick up his kill, he saw that he was in the middle of the forbidden Valley of Grief. And suddenly, he felt his heart wrung by a strange longing.

When he returned that day from the hunt with his head hanging down the fairy sisters knew at once where he had been.

"What is the matter, Valiant?" his wife asked him.

"I don't know, my dear," replied the Prince, "but I suddenly feel a desperate longing in my heart. I would like go home and see my family once more!"

"Ah, you poor unfortunate one!" cried the fairy sisters. "You were in the Valley of Grief, weren't you?"

"I was," admitted Prince Valliant, "but I swear I did not go there on purpose."

And he told the sisters what had happened. "Ever since then I long to see my mother and father. Ever since then I have thought of nothing else but seeing my home once more," he said finally. Let me go there for a few days, and I shall return again gladly."

"Do not go, Valiant," the fairy sisters pleaded. "Time here goes more slowly than it does for ordinary people. In the short time you have seen with us, whole centuries have gone by outside. Your family is long since in their grave, and if you go back into world, you will almost certainly never return. Stay here with us!"

But Prince Valiant would not be persuaded. Neither the fairy sisters, nor his own wife, nor even his faithful winged horse could convince him to stay.

"Believe what I say," the horse told him. "I'm afraid that you'll never return to us."

"I will return, old fellow," replied Prince Valiant. "Take me home for just a few hours and than I shall come back gladly. Otherwise I should die here of grief and suffering."

"Very well," said the faithful horse at last, "but when we get there and you dismount, I shall wait for you only one hour, no more, and then if you don't come back to me, I must return, even without you."

"I shall come back, faithful horse, I shall come back," said the Prince joyfully, and he began to prepare for the journey.

They set off the next day at dawn. Prince Valiant said farewell to the fairy sisters, kissed his wife goodbye, spurred his faithful horse and was gone.

"Farewell!" the three fairy sisters cried after him with tears in their eyes. "Come back to us soon!" But Prince Valiant was already far away and did not hear them.

The journey went by swiftly and Prince Valiant could hardly believe what he saw. Although he had come this way only a year ago, as he thought, everything was quite changed. There, where once the lonely domain of the Dragon Crone lay, now towered a wealthy city surrounded by villages and fields, and where once the palace of the Owl Crone stood, now gleamed the capital of a huge kingdom. And when from time to time Valiant would stop and ask passers-by about something, they would only shake their heads and say, "The Dragon Crone? The Owl Crone? Why they exist only in children's fairy tales!" And they would laugh in his face as though he were mad.

And so Prince Valiant finally arrived at the city where his father the King had once ruled. Valiant still recognized the city, but he never found the palace where he was born. All that remained of it was a ruin, here a crumbled tower, there the remnants of a gate, and underneath it all a few collapsed cellars.

Prince Valiant jumped down from his horse, took him by the bridle and led him into what was once the court-yard. The winged horse said, "There, you see my Lord? Everything is long since gone and passed away, and your family too. Come, jump into the saddle and let's be away. Your hour is almost up. Otherwise, I must return alone."

But Prince Valiant couldn't bring himself to leave yet. "Go back alone, faithful fellow, if you must" he said. "I want to look around just a little longer."

And the winged horse whinneyed sadly and then flew off like an arrow the way he had come.

Prince Valiant watched him for as long as he could keep him in his sight, and then he began to walk through the ruins again. He walked about for a long time, but he could find nothing which brought him any pleasure. All that former magnificence was now just a heap of stones. And the longer Prince Valiant walked, the heavier his steps became, the more stooped his back became, the heavier his eyelids seemed, the whiter and longer the hair on his head and the beard on his chin grew, until all at once, he felt as though he were a thousand years old. And just then, in the corner of a half-collapsed cellar, he saw an old chest. It was the very chest where once he had found the weapons his father had used when he was young.

"I wonder what is in it now?" he said, opening the trunk. And from the depths of the chest there came a quiet voice which said, "Welcome, Valiant! I have been waiting for you a thousand years, and if you hadn't come today, it would have been the end of me forever."

Prince Valiant was astonished. "Who are you," he said, "that you know me and that you have waited for me for so long?"

And the quiet voice answered, "I am your death."

And then someone laid a hand on Valiant's shoulders and with a sigh, the Prince changed on the spot into a pile of dust which the gentle wind scattered among the ruins.

And so the fairy sisters, in their palace of youth without age and life without death, never saw Prince Valiant again. All that was left to them was their memory of him, and this tale, nothing more.

WILLIE WAS SOMEWHAT SLEEPY. *All morning his eyes had been wanting to shut by themselves, and Granny finally noticed it. She felt his forehead. "Don't tell me you've got a fever again, laddie?" she said.*

And just to be sure, she put him to bed immediately after lunch. Willie was asleep almost before his head touched the pillow. He dreamed that he was Prince Valiant and that he had set off to free a beautiful Princess. The Princess had golden hair and eyes like dark pools, but she was very small, just like the little girl from the fireplace. When Prince Valiant set her free, there was a wedding and a huge banquet with potatoes roasted in the oven. That was what Willie liked best of all.

"Come on, up you get Willie. They are ready," called Granny, interrupting his dreams.

Willie woke up remembering that he really had asked her to bake some potatoes for him, and he ran quickly to the kitchen. By his appetite, Granny was certain that he didn't have a fever.

Willie secretly took one baked potato back to his room with him. It was still warm that evening when he offered it to the little girl from the fireplace. She found it very tasty but a half was enough for her. From the second half she used her magic to make a plump little boat which sailed over the bearskin rug as though it were sailing over the sea. But on the far shore of that sea it suddenly tumbled into the floor and once again it was just a half-eaten potato.

Then the little girl said to Willie, "Now read to me!"

Willie eagerly opened the book and very slowly and with plenty of expression, he began to read. And this is what he read.

THE SORCERER WITH THREE IRON HOOPS

Once upon a time there was a King and that King had a son. When the Prince grew up and was old enough to marry, the King summoned him and said, "Son, it is time for you to find a bride, and I would like to know her before I close my eyes forever. I would like to have grandchildren before they lay me to rest."

The Prince had no objections to a wedding. "I'd be very happy to marry, Father," he said, "but I don't know where to find a bride."

"It's a very simple matter," said the old King, and he pulled a golden key out of his pocket and handed it to the Prince.

"Take this key," he said, "and go to the castle tower. At the very top there is a chamber with as many windows as there are days in the year. In every window there is a portrait of a beautiful and eligible young princess. Look them over well, and then come and tell me which one of them you would like."

The Prince was truly surprised, for this was the first time he had ever heard of this room with the pictures of the princesses. Quickly he took the key, nimbly he ran up the tower staircase, and soon he was standing before its heavy iron door. When he touched the door with the golden key, it swung open and the Prince gasped in amazement.

Before his eyes lay a magnificent room, full of gold and silver and precious stones, and all around the room there were exactly three hundred and sixty-six windows. And in every window, there was a beautiful princess with a crown on her head, and each one was looking at the Prince.

As if in a dream, the good Prince went from one princess to the next, bowing to each one and greeting each one, and each one smiled back at him in reply. They were all beautiful and he liked every one of them very much, but whenever he imagined one of them as his wife, he shook his head and went on to the next. And so he went round the whole room, until finally he came to the last window. It was covered with a thick veil, but in spite of this, there flowed from it such a light that the Prince could not resist. Fearlessly he flung back the veil and then stood frozen to the spot. For underneath there was a princess, but so beautiful and so sweet and so sad that his heart almost stopped in his chest.

The Prince's mind was made up in a moment. "It is you I want, and none other!" he said.

No sooner had he said this than the princess blushed, lowered her eyes, and disappeared. And in the very same moment, all the other princesses disappeared too.

The Prince returned to his father the King. "Well, which one did you choose?" the old man asked him.

"The most beautiful and the most unhappy," answered the Prince, "the one hidden behind the veil."

The old King was alarmed. "What have you done, my son?" he cried. "Why did you cast aside the veil? Now certain death awaits you. That princess is in the power of a sorcerer with three iron hoops, and everyone who has tried to set her free has perished. And you will perish too! Put her out of your mind, I beg of you!"

But the Prince could not forget the princess behind the veil. "I want her and none other," he told his father. "If I cannot have her, I shall surely perish of grief. And therefore I pray you, let me go and find her. Perhaps I shall have better luck than the others."

The King did not want to let his son go, but the Prince pleaded and begged for so long that the old man finally gave his consent. And so he bade farewell to his father, mounted his horse, and gaily set forth to find his princess.

He searched for a long, long time, riding all alone, until one day he lost his way in the middle of a deep forest. Just when he thought that he would never find his way out, he saw a very strange fellow on the edge of a clearing, sitting in the cool shade of a tree. He had hands and feet like great branches, and his head was lost somewhere in the crown of the tree.

"Hello, friend," the Prince called to him. "Do you by any chance know the way out of these woods?"

"I don't," replied the tall fellow, "but I can take a look."

He stood up and began to stretch himself until his head touched the clouds, then he looked around on all sides and shouted down at the Prince, "The edge of the woods is straight ahead, sir! It's just a stone's throw and a short ride away."

And then the tall fellow made himself shorter again, until he was no bigger than the Prince on his horse.

The Prince was amazed, for never had he seen anything like it in his life.

"What do they call you?" he asked. "And where are you off to?"

"They call me Tall," answered the fellow, "and I'm going into the world to look for adventure."

"Then come along with me," said the Prince, and Tall nodded eagerly in agreement.

"With pleasure, sir, for two always travel better than one," he replied.

And then he took the Prince's horse by the bridle and led them out of the woods.

At the edge of the woods, they saw another fellow under a tree. He had a belly like a barrel, a head like a tub and hands and feet like pumpkins.

"Hello, friend," the Prince called to him. "What are you doing here?"

"What am I doing?" replied the fat fellow. "Why I'm waiting for a man with whom I can go into the world and look for adventure."

"And what do they call you?" asked the Prince.

"They call me Broad," answered the fellow, "because I can stretch myself in all directions like no one else in the world. Just watch."

And Broad opened his mouth and began to huff and puff and his belly swelled up in all directions like a mountain. The Prince had to step smartly to get out of his way. Never had he seen anything like it in his life before.

"Come with me, then," he said to the fellow, and Broad nodded eagerly in agreement.

"With pleasure, sir, for three always travel better than two," he replied.

And so he took the Prince's horse by the bridle on the other side and the three of them went merrily on. Before long they saw a third fellow on the road ahead of them. He was walking towards them with a scarf over his eyes.

"Hello, friend," the Prince called to him. "What are you doing?"

"What am I doing?" replied the fellow with the scarf over his eyes. "I'm looking for a man with whom I can go into the world and look for adventure."

"And what do they call you?" asked the Prince.

"They call me Sharp-eyes," replied the fellow, "because I can see everything in the world, even if it's hidden deep in the rocks or on the bottom of the sea. And that's why I wear this scarf over my eyes. If I didn't wear it, everything I looked at would fly into little pieces. Just watch."

And he took the scarf off and fixed his eyes upon a rock by the side of the road. As soon as he looked at it, the rock collapsed into a heap of pebbles and sand.

The Prince was amazed, for he had never seen anything like this in his life. "Then come with me," he said to the fellow, and Sharp-eyes nodded in agreement.

"With pleasure," he replied. "The four of us can take on the whole world. But tell me, where are you off to?"

"I am looking for the castle of a sorcerer with three iron hoops," replied the Prince. "He has a beautiful princess in his power, and I mean that princess to be my bride. Do you know where the castle lies?"

"That we do not," replied Sharp-eyes for all of them, "but we can have a look round for it."

And without another word, he took the scarf off his eyes and looked all around the world. On the midnight side, in the middle of a deep forest, he saw a black castle and in that castle, in a tower, behind an iron grate, sat the fair princess.

"I see where the castle is, sir," cried Sharp-eyes, "and I can see your bride. We must go straight towards midnight. If you were to travel there alone, it would take you a year. But with us, you'll be there in a day."

And sure enough, early next day they stood before the black castle belonging to the sorcerer with three hoops. The castle stood on a high rock, with its black towers touching the clouds, and its gate was closed. When they pounded on it, no one opened, and when they called, no one answered.

"Then you will have to open it for us," said the Prince to Sharp-eyes.

Sharp-eyes did not wait to be asked a second time. He removed his scarf, fixed his eyes upon the gate and the gate swung open. The Prince and his three friends entered the court-yard, but the courtyard was empty: there was not a living soul to be seen.

"Hallo, is anyone here?" called the Prince.

"Hallo there, come and greet four tired wanderers!" called the Prince's companions, but not a sound, not a footfall, not a voice could be heard anywhere. But in the stable they discovered a manger full of hay awaiting their horse, and in the dining hall a richly laid table welcomed them. The Prince and his companions sat down at the table and ate and drank their fill and then began to look around for a place to sleep for the night. Suddenly the door of the hall flew open and on the threshold stood the lord of the castle. It was the sorcerer with three hoops. His eyes blazed like two flames of fire, his white beard was tangled like a cluster of snakes, and around his waist he wore three bands of iron. He was leading an exquisitely beautiful princess by the hand. She was the same princess the Prince had seen in the window behind the heavy veil.

The Prince wanted to run up to her, but the sorcerer stopped him. "I know why you have come," he said, "and you can have what you desire. If you succeed in keeping watch over your bride for three nights, she is yours. But if you fail, you and your servants shall pay for it with your heads!"

And then he seated the princess in a golden chair and left the room.

The Prince could hardly take his eyes off the beautiful princess. He gazed at her and spoke to her without ceasing, but she did not reply. She merely stared sadly ahead as though she were made of stone. Finally the Prince too fell silent, sat down opposite her, and began to keep watch.

The Prince and his three helpers stood watch, but they could not last the whole night. At about midnight, their heads began to droop and in a little while all four were sleeping like logs. When the first light of dawn began to appear outside the window, the Prince jumped up in alarm, for he saw that the golden chair was empty!

"Wake up, wake up!" he cried to his companions, "A terrible thing has happened! The princess has gone!"

Sharp-eyes rubbed his eyes and said, "There's nothing to worry about, sir. I shall find her."

And he looked about in all directions and then cried out, "I see her! I know where she is! A hundred miles away there is a huge rock in a forest and on that rock there is an eagle's nest and in that nest there is an egg. That is the princess. Tall, take me there!"

Tall lifted Sharp-eyes on his shoulder, took one huge step, and then another, and with the third step they were at the rock. Sharp-eyes climbed into the eagle's nest and took the egg, and then they started back. Before the sun appeared on the horizon, they handed the egg to the Prince. When he dropped it on the ground, the princess in all her beauty stood before him once more and her sad face lit up with happiness when she recognized him.

But the sorcerer frowned like a thunder cloud when he came into the room and saw the princess, and he was in such a fit of anger that one of the iron hoops around his waist burst.

"Very well, Prince," he fumed, "you have managed to watch over the princess once. But we shall see how you fare a second time!"

And he led the princess away to her chambers in a rage.

The Prince and his friends spent the whole day walking through the castle and its gardens. Everywhere they found unheard of riches — gold, silver, and precious stones — until their eyes were tired from the splendour of it all.

At noon, a mid-day meal awaited them on the dining-room table, and in the evening, a generous supper also was prepared for them. Just when they were looking around for a place to lie down for the night, the door flew open and the lord of the castle stood on the threshold. He had two iron hoops around his waist and he was leading the exquisitely beautiful princess by the hand. Again the Prince wanted to run up to her, but the sorcerer stopped him.

"Stay where you are, Prince," he said sternly. "First you must prove that you are worthy of the princess. If you keep watch over her for two more nights, she is yours. But as I have told you, if you fail, you shall pay with your head."

And then he seated the princess in the golden chair and left.

The Prince couldn't take his eyes off the beautiful princess. Once again he spoke to her unceasingly, but the princess did not reply. She remained silent, as if she were made of stone. And finally the Prince too fell silent, and he sat down opposite her and began to keep watch.

The Prince and his three helpers stood watch, but not even this time were they able to stay awake the whole night. Around midnight, their eyes suddenly became very heavy and in a little while all four of them were sleeping like logs. When the first light of dawn began to come through the window, the Prince awoke abruptly and to his utter dismay, the golden chair was empty again.

"Wake up, wake up!" he shouted to his companions. "The princess has gone again!"

Sharp-eyes rubbed his eyes and said, "There's nothing to worry about, sir, I shall find her."

And then he looked around in every direction and finally he cried, "I see her now! I know where she is! Five hundred miles from here there is a field of wheat and on the edge of that field a stalk of wheat is growing and at the very top of that stalk there is a seed. That seed is our princess. Tall, take me there!"

Tall lifted Sharp-eyes on his shoulders, took four huge steps and at the fifth, they were in the field of wheat. Sharp-eyes pulled up the stalk, took out the seed and then they started back. Before the sun appeared on the horizon, they were back in the castle. They handed the grain of wheat to the Prince, and when he dropped it on the ground, the princess in all her beauty, stood before him and her sad face shone once more with happiness.

But when the sorcerer came into the room and saw the princess there once more, he frowned like a thunder-cloud, and the second iron hoop around his waist burst from sheer anger. "Very well, Prince," he snarled, "You have managed to watch over the princess twice. We shall see how you fare a third time!"

And he led the princess back to her chambers.

The Prince and his companions spent the whole day once more walking around the castle and its gardens. At noon they had a fine lunch and in the evening they ate a delicious supper, and just when they were looking round for a place to sleep for the night, the door flew open and the lord of the castle stood on the threshold.

Around his waist he had the third and last iron hoop and he led the exquisitely beautiful princess by the hand. For the third time the Prince wanted to run up and embrace her, but the sorcerer stopped him.

"Stay where you are, Prince," he said. "First you must show that you are worthy of your bride and keep watch over her for one more night. If you are successful, she is yours, but if not, be prepared to meet your death."

And then he seated the princess in the golden chair and left.

The Prince sat and gazed at the princess, but not even this time could he encourage her to speak or bring her to smile. She was as silent as a stone, and finally the Prince stopped trying and had to content himself with keeping watch over her.

The Prince and his three friends stood watch, but once again, by midnight, all four of them were fast asleep. It wasn't until the day began to appear beyond the window that the Prince awoke in a terrible fright. The golden chair was empty for the third time.

"Wake up! Wake up!" he shouted to his three companions. "It's happened again! The princess is gone."

Sharp-eyes rubbed his eyes and said, "There's nothing to be afraid of, sir, I shall find her."

For a long time, he looked around in every direction but at last he cried, "I see her! I know where she is! A thousand miles from here, in the mountains, there is a lake, and on the bottom of the lake there is a shell, and in that shell there is a pearl. And that pearl is our princess. Tall, take me there quickly, and take Broad as well, for we shall need him."

Tall took Sharp-eyes on one shoulder and Broad on the other and started off and in one, two, ten long strides he was at the lake. He set Broad down on the shore and Broad started to work at once. He began to drink the water and he drank so quickly that the bottom soon appeared. Then Sharp-eyes found the shell with the pearl inside easily, and with the pearl in their hands, they rushed back to the castle.

And it wasn't a moment too soon; for the sun was just peeking over the horizon, the door to the Prince's room was just creaking open, and still there was no princess. At the very last moment, just when the sorcerer was standing on the threshold, a pearl flew in through the open window and as soon as it touched the floor, the Prince's beautiful bride stood before him and her face shone like the sun.

No sooner had the sorcerer laid eyes on the princess than his third iron hoop burst and the sorcerer changed into a black raven on the spot.

And at that very moment a tremendous hubbub began as though the whole castle were collapsing around them, and when the noise died down, they could hear joyous peals of laughter echoing all around them. From all sides, lords and knights came rushing happily up to the Prince and the princess. The evil sorcerer had placed them all under a spell and the Prince and his three companions had set them free.

And what happened next, you ask? Well, all that remained now was a grand wedding, and at that wedding the good Prince married his beloved princess. The three odd fellows, Tall, Broad and Sharp-eyes were the best men, and when the wedding was over, the Prince asked them to act as his counsellors. They thanked him for the honour but refused, because they wanted to go into the world again and look for more adventure. And so the Prince sent them off with his thanks and ever afterward he told his children and his grandchildren how he set out to find his bride and how he had been helped by Tall, Broad and Sharp-eyes.

IT WASN'T UNTIL HE HAD FINISHED READING
that Willie noticed what the little girl from the fireplace was
doing. From the uneaten half of her baked potato, from the
old, shipwrecked boat, she had kneaded three little figures and
now these figures were marching through the forest of the bear-
skin rug towards the fireplace. The first one was tall and thin,
the second was round and stout, and the third one had a scarf
over his eyes. And when the three of them reached the hearth,
a burning log crackled and the wanderers were surrounded by
a crowd of fiery little men. And all together, they began to
dance, and they danced and danced until they finally disap-
peared in a whirlwind up the chimney.

All this made Willie begin to see spots before his eyes. Even if
he had wanted to, he could read no longer. So he simply wait-
ed.

The little girl didn't make him wait long. She put her finger
to her lips as she always did, so that he would be silent and
listen and as usual, he heard the still, quiet voice of the Wind
coming from the chimney. And this is the story she told.

TWO BROTHERS AND THREE MIRRORS

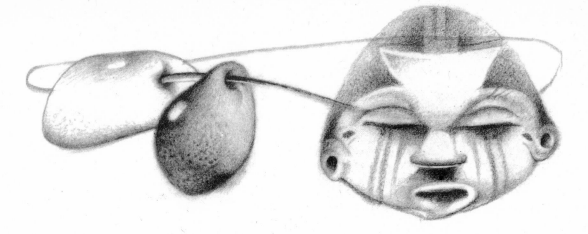

Once upon a time, long ago, there lived a woman and she gave birth to two little twin boys. They were as alike as two eggs, as two pebbles, as two stars, and she gave them two nice names, Tumba and Vunga. But two nice names was all she could give them. She had nothing else because she was very, very poor.

The woman was poor, but she wanted her twin sons to have happiness and good fortune, and so she went into the wilderness to seek out a certain magician.

"Oh wise man," she said to him, "I have two sons — twins, and I want them to have happiness and good fortune forever. Can you tell me how?"

The magician could and did. He took two pebbles, each with a hole through the centre, gave them to the mother and said, "Here are two powerful talismans. As long as your sons wear them around their necks, happiness and good fortune will follow them wherever they go. Go and give them to them."

The woman thanked the magician for the talismans, returned home with them, and hung them around her sons necks. And the boys grew like spring grass! Day by day they grew sturdier and more handsome and more clever. No one else in the village had ever had such fine sons. In short, they were the kind of young men any woman would be glad to marry.

One day Tumba went to his mother and said, "Mother, the time has come for me to go into the world and try my luck."

His mother nodded and said, "Go, my son. My blessings go with you, and may you have a safe return!"

Tumba said farewell to his mother, took leave of his brother, and left the town. Just outside the town gates a tall, leafy tree was growing beside the road. Tumba broke off two green shoots from its branches, touched them with his powerful talisman, and said,

"My powerful talisman, I need a horse and I need a knife. Or do you want me to go into the world unmounted and unarmed?"

The powerful talisman gave Tumba everything he wanted. No sooner had he thrown the shoots down than a horse stood before him. No sooner had they fallen in the dust of the road than he had a knife in his belt. And then Tumba mounted the horse and set off into the world.

When evening came, he brought his horse to a halt in a rocky wilderness. He was hungry and thirsty and there was not a sign of human habitation anywhere. Tumba picked up a stone and touched it with his powerful talisman and said, "Oh talisman, I am hungry and thirsty and so is my horse. Or do you want us to die at the beginning of our journey?"

And then he threw the stone down. No sooner had it touched the ground than a mat lay before him spread with food and drink, and there was food and water for his horse as well. When they had satisfied their hunger and thirst, they lay down and slept, and in the morning, they awoke with the sun and went on their way.

And so Tumba went through the world on his good horse and together they saw many countries and many cities. One day, he saw battlements on the horizon, and beyond the battlements towered a city. The city was ruled over by a rich King, and this King had a beautiful daughter. Many a young man had paid court to her and many a wealthy lord wanted to marry her, but the Princess would have no one. They all said that she was too proud, for she always kept her face hidden behind a veil.

Though she showed her face to no one, she showed it to Tumba almost at once. For when Tumba rode up to the city walls, he stopped his horse by the river to let him drink. Just then the King's daughter happened to be walking by ard as soon as she saw him, she felt a sharp pain in her heart. So sick with love was she that she could scarcely walk home.

When she arrived home she went before her father and said, "Oh my Father, I have just met a stranger by the river, and my heart is so sore with love that I could scarcely walk home. I want him for my husband, and if he will not be mine, it will be my death."

The King was frightened and overjoyed all at once. He was frightened to think that his daughter might die, and he was overjoyed that at last she wanted to marry. He sent nis guard for the stranger, and when the guard brought Tumba back to the castle, the King saw that his daughter had chosen well. And he held a banquet in honour of the unexpected guest.

The unexpected guest accepted the invitation and he brought the King kingly gifts. He took a handful of pebbles from the ground, touched them with his powerful talisman, and said, "Oh my talisman, the King has invited me to dine with him. I must have gifts for him. Or do you want me to appear before him like a beggar?"

And then he threw the pebbles on the ground. No sooner had they fallen than the ground before him lay strewn with precious gifts for the King. When Tumba brought them to him, the King saw that his daughter had chosen well, for such a bridegroom was truly hard to find. And with no further ado he offered Tumba his beautiful daughter, and the welcoming banquet became a wedding feast.

After the wedding, the Princess took her new husband to her house. The Princess's house was very large and very beautiful. Each room in it was more magnificent than the one before. In the very last room, three large mirrors hung on the wall, each one covered with a curtain, but though Tumba was very curious, he said nothing the first day. The second day he was also silent, but the third day he could hold back no longer and he said, "Tell me, my beloved, why are those mirrors always hidden with a curtain?"

"Do not ask, my darling," replied the Princess a little anxiously. "Those mirrors have magic power; they hold their own secrets and whoever shall know those secrets will regret it."

But Tumba paid no attention to the warning. "Show me at least one of them, my dear," he said. "Throw back the curtain so that I may have a look."

"Then look if you must, my darling," said the Princess sadly. "Look into the first mirror. You will see the town where you were born. But do not ask to see any more."

And the Princess cast aside the curtain covering the first mirror and Tumba saw his native town as though he were looking at it through a window. Everywhere he saw familiar houses, familiar streets, and the familiar faces of friends and relations. Tumba felt a sharp pang of longing and homesickness in his heart and he wanted to see more.

"Show me the second mirror too, my beloved," he said. "Pull back the curtain so I may look."

"Then look if you must, my darling," said the Princess sadly. "Look into my second mirror and you will see all the cities you have passed through. But do not ask to see more."

And the Princess cast aside the curtain covering the second mirror and Tumba saw there all the cities which he had passed through, full of houses and streets, and everywhere there were faces both familiar and unknown. Tumba felt another sharp pain of longing and desire in his heart and he wanted to see still more.

"Show me the third mirror as well, my beloved," he pleaded. "Cast aside the curtain and let me look."

But the Princess would not pull back the curtain and said, "Do not ask me to do this, my darling. Do not look into the third mirror. For there you will see the city from which there is no return."

And so Tumba himself stretched out his hand and flung back the curtain covering the third mirror and looked. In the mirror, he saw a city deserted and empty, as though the wind had rushed through and carried away every living thing. As soon as Tumba saw the city he felt a sharp pain in his heart and he said, "I must see this city with my own eyes, my beloved. If I do not, it will be my death."

Without delay, he jumped onto his horse and set off to find the city he had seen in the mirror. Long he searched, long he rode through the world, long he journeyed ever forward on his horse, until at last he came to a land of sand and rock.

Everywhere there was desolation and emptiness, and only the sun blazed down on that terrible desert. In the middle of the desert stood a city of black and white stone. It was the city he had seen in the third mirror. At the gates of the city sat an old crone, as old as the stones themselves and as cruel as the desert. She held a green wand in her hand. Tumba was glad to see a human; in fact he was so overjoyed to meet a living soul, that he jumped down from his horse, leaving his powerful talisman behind. And the wicked old woman, who was an evil old witch, gave Tumba a flick with her green wand and the stalwart young man and his faithful horse changed into black stones on the spot.

While Tumba was lying by the city in the desert as a black stone, his brother Vunga was waiting at home for him. When six months had gone by and his brother had not yet returned, when a year had passed and there was no news of him, Vunga went to his mother and said, "The time has come for me to go into the world and try my luck. The time has come for me to find my brother Tumba."

His mother nodded and said, "Go, my son, and my blessings go with you. May you fare well, and return safely with your brother."

And so Vunga, too, said farewell to his mother and left the town. Just outside the town gates a tall leafy tree was growing beside the road. Vunga broke off two green shoots, touched them with his talisman, and said, "Oh my powerful talisman, I need a horse and I need a knife. Or do you want me to go into the world unmounted and unarmed?"

And the powerful talisman gave Vunga everything he wanted. No sooner had he thrown the shoots down than a horse stood before him. No sooner had they fallen into the dust of the road than he had a knife in the belt around his waist. And so Vunga set out into the world to look for his brother, and so he came to the city where Tumba had married a year before. When Vunga rode into the city and through the streets, the people called out happily to him, "Welcome, Tumba, our dear Prince. Welcome back from your long journey. Your wife has been anxiously awaiting your return."

Vunga saw that the people thought he was his brother and he knew from what they said that his brother had married in this city. The people took him to the house of the beautiful Princess.

"Come out, Princess," they called. "Your husband has returned!"

And the Princess came out of the house and welcomed Vunga as her own husband.

"Where have you been so long, my darling?" she said. "No more shall you look into my mirrors, for if you did, you would surely go off again and perhaps you would never return."

But Vunga wanted to see the magic mirrors, for he wanted to see where his brother had gone. And when he looked into the three mirrors, when he saw the city from which there is no return, he knew without being told where to look for his brother. He ran out of the house, jumped onto his horse, and urging it on, he cried out to the Princess, "Now I know where to look for my brother Tumba."

And then the Princess knew that it was not Tumba. She knew that it must be his brother, and that he, too, was going to the city from which there is no return.

Vunga travelled through the world for a long time until he too came to that desolate land of rock and sand where the city from the third mirror stood. At the gate sat the old crone, as old as the rocks around her and as cruel as the desert, and she held the green wand in her hand.

Although Vunga was glad to see a human being, and indeed was overjoyed to see a living soul, he was careful. He didn't jump down from his horse. He took hold of his powerful talisman, and well he did so! For when the old crone flicked him with her green wand, the stalwart young man remained what he was, and his horse likewise. But as for the old woman, she changed into a rock.

No sooner had the old witch changed into a rock than the desolate city suddenly came alive, and people rushed towards Vunga from all sides. Leading them was his brother Tumba. The brothers embraced one another joyously and then set out happily for home to rejoin Tumba's wife, the beautiful princess and her father. When they arrived, everyone was amazed at what had happened to them, but what amazed them most was how much the brothers looked alike. Even the princess found it difficult to tell them apart. And then the King held a great celebration and he entrusted the brothers with his city and his crown. And from that time on, they all lived in happiness and good fortune and their mother lived happily with them.

And what about the three mirrors? When the brothers stepped into the room where they had once hung, when they went to see what the mirrors would show now, the mirrors were gone, all three of them. But this did not spoil their happiness.

NEXT MORNING GRANNY GREETED WILLIE WITH A QUESTION.

"Willie, who is it you're always talking to in the evenings? Or are you talking in your sleep?"

The question caught Willie by surprise and he hardly knew what to reply. Finally he said, "I'm reading to myself."

It was true, after all. But Granny wanted to know more. "And you read out loud?"

"Yes," replied Willie.

Even that was true too. But Granny still wasn't satisfied. "And can you see well enough to read?"

"Of course!" said Willie. "There's enough light from the fireplace."

And Grannie smiled and said only "Aha", and then she went to cook dinner. But that evening she brought Willie a little lamp to his room and said, "This is so you'll see better, if you feel like reading out loud again."

And then she kissed Willie and closed the door behind her.

That evening the little girl from the fireplace was especially active. She wanted to play tag and hide-and-seek, while Willie could only whisper, "Quiet! Be quiet! Granny heard us last night. Come on, I'll read you something really nice."

And so the little girl sat down on the head of the bear-skin rug and Willie began to read slowly and very quietly. And this is what he read:

THE SLEEPING BEAUTY

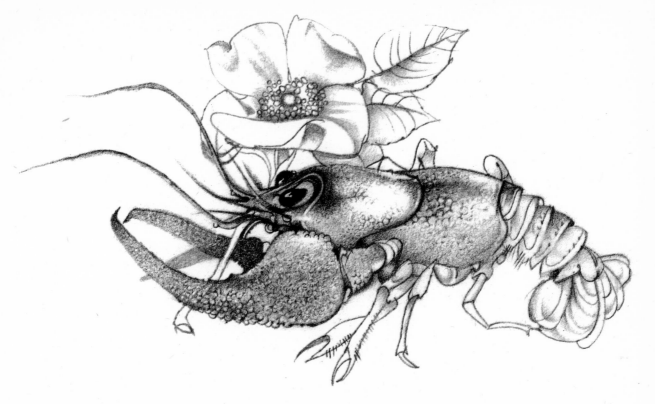

Once upon a time there lived a King who ruled happily with his Queen, a woman as beautiful as a flower and the envy of all the world. One thing however, marred their happiness: the King and the Queen were childless. For years they waited, all in vain, until the Queen could scarcely bear the misery, and in her deep distress, she'd wander sadly through the garden, seeking consolation in the flowers.

One day, while she was sitting by the pool, the still water was ruffled by a gentle breeze and suddenly, a huge crab surfaced from the deep. Looking at the Queen it said, "I know your sorrow, dear lady, but you shall weep no more, for in a year and a day, you shall have a child, a daughter!" And then it disappeared beneath the water.

And as the crab had said, in a year and a day the Queen took to her bed and gave birth to a lovely child, a daughter, both beautiful and gentle.

Both King and Queen were overjoyed. Their happiness was now unmarred, and, as was the custom in his land, the King declared a holiday of feasting and revelry, and he gave a grand feast to celebrate the birth. And to this feast, along with others of his family, he summoned twelve good fairies to be godmothers to his first-born child.

As soon as the feast was in full swing, and the King and Queen were sparkling and happy, the fairies came, borne through the door on the gentle evening air. The guests looked on bemused while, one by one, the fairies came up to the child and gave her gifts befitting a fair princess. The first one gave her lovely golden hair, the second eyes of deepest blue, the third rose-red lips, the fourth wished her happiness in love, and so they continued, until the twelfth and last stepped up to give the child her present.

But as she bent above the princess, the door flew open and a bitter gust of wind blew out the candles. No one uttered a word. All hearts turned cold, for there, standing on the threshold, her face twisted in a wicked leer, stood an evil witch, as old as the very world and with a heart as black as night. The hag had come without an invitation, and both King and Queen paled as they saw her, for they knew well that this unwanted visitation could bring no good.

All were powerless to stop her. The guests fell back as if entranced to let the evil fairy through, and in a moment the ugly crone was by the child's side. In tones of ice, she said, "The King, your father, did not summon me, but I have come myself, and I have brought a special gift for you. When sixteen winters have passed, when you are the apple of your parent's eye, you shall prick your finger upon a spindle and draw your final breath. For that prick shall be the prick of death!"

With these words, the old hag disappeared — even before the King could call his guard and have her banished from the feast. The poor Queen sank into a swoon from terror, but the last good fairy went to the baby. Gently rocking the cradle, she said, "Fear not, sweet child, let not your parents be afraid. I shall not let you come to harm, for when you prick your finger, you shall not die, but merely fall into such a deep sleep that it will last three hundred years. When three centuries have gone by, you shall be awakened by a kiss and evermore shall live in love and happiness."

With that, the fairies departed, before the King and Queen could give their heart-felt thanks, and before the guests could say a word.

But though the kind fairies vanished, their gifts remained behind. The princess grew, and as she grew, she became more and more charming and beautiful, until she was truly a flower of the human race. Her face was fair, her lips like rose-buds and her hair was golden as the sun.

As every day the Princess grew more lovely, so every day the King's heart grew heavier. He could not sleep at night, and he could scarcely eat or drink by day. All his efforts were directed to find a way to break the witch's evil spell and to keep his darling child from harm.

At last he hit upon a plan. He sent his heralds throughout the land to issue a decree which stated that on pain of death all spinning wheels must be destroyed. In addition said that no more thread or yarn of any kind could be used.

The spinners and weavers in the kingdom were extremely troubled, and since they could no longer earn their daily bread, they left the land, still puzzling over the decree. The King however, felt great relief and convinced that his daughter was now safe, he once more ate and drank and slept easily.

But while the King and Queen rejoiced that the danger was over, the evil fairy was merely waiting for a chance to work her wickedness. Sure enough as the Princess turned sixteen that chance came. On the day of her birthday, the King and Queen were walking

106

in the palace garden, and the Princess was alone in the castle. She wandered through the great rooms, looking at the pictures on the walls, when all at once, at the end of a long corridor, she came upon a heavy wooden door.

"That's odd," the Princess thought, "I've never noticed that before."

Just then, as if by magic, the door swung open and the Princess saw the strangest thing. For in the middle of the room, all alone, an ugly crone sat spinning at a spinning-wheel, and as she spun, she sang this song:

"Spin, my little wheel, spin,
Wind, my little bobbin, wind.
Please do your best for our sweet guest,
A maid both fair and kind."

Though the Princess was alarmed by the old woman, she was charmed by the song she sang.

"Come in my dear", the old hag said. "There's no reason to be afraid. Come in, and you may try it too."

The Princess had never seen a spinning-wheel before and, as if in a trance, she stepped through the door and took the spindle which the old woman offered her. But alas, no sooner had the spindle touched her hand than the Princess felt a prick of pain. Immediately darkness engulfed her and she sank into a deep, deep sleep.

The old crone's spell left no one in the palace untouched, for in that very moment, the self-same darkness descended on the castle and everything around. The King and Queen, returning from the garden, fell sound asleep upon the staircase, while their train of lords and ladies, in all their courtly dress, slumped to the ground in deep unconsciousness. And stable-boys and chamber maids, cooks over their pots and guards-at-arm, all fell victim to the witch's evil spell. Even the hounds in the yard, the horses in their stables, and the flies on the walls slept a sleep as sound as death.

The countryside around them slept too. Soon roads and pathways to the castle were overgrown with bushes and briars, weeds and vines, until the forest round the castle was so thick no mortal man would dare to enter it. Very soon, hardly a man alive remembered that a magnificent castle had stood proudly in the middle of that forbidding forest.

So the years went by, and gradually turned into centuries. When three hundred years had passed since sleep had locked the land in timelessness, a young and dashing prince came there to hunt. Suddenly he found the road he had been following vanished into that tangled and impenetrable forest. He stopped his horse abruptly, for he could not believe his eyes.

Just then, an old man came wandering by and so the good prince questioned him. "Tell me, old man, what forest is this that swallows up the very road I ride upon?"

The old man answered, "By the white hairs on this old head, I know nothing but what the legends say."

"And what might that be, old man?" asked the prince.

"Well", the old man replied, "it is said that on this spot where the forest now grows, there once stood a palace where a wealthy King lived with his Queen and lovely daughter. But the Princess has been sleeping now for three hundred years and will sleep on until the day she is awakened by a kiss. So say the legends."

"Then by my sword and by my youth, old man, I shall find her and awaken her", said the prince boldly, and without another word, he spurred his horse into the forest.

And then it seemed as if a miracle was happening. The wood opened up as if to welcome him and urge him on. Thorn and vine and briar and bush fell back to make a path and soon the good Prince found himself before the slumbering palace. At first he thought it was a dream. The guards-in-arm, the horses in their stables, the dogs in the yard and the flies on the walls were all sound asleep. Even the King and Queen were asleep on the staircase where the charm had caught them.

The prince entered the palace doors and walked through endless corridors thick with the dust of three hundred years. He looked through every room, explored each chamber, until at last he came to a huge wooden door which swung open as if to invite him inside. And there, lying upon a bed, was a beautiful princess.

The prince's heart stopped beating for an instant, for so still she lay there that he was sure she must be dead. But when he got close to her, and saw how red her lips were, he was unable to resist. Bending over, he reached down and kissed her. As soon as their lips touched, the princess opened her eyes and looked at him: the spell was broken. For with her, the whole castle had awoken. The guards began their pacing back and forth, the hounds in the yard began to bark, the horses whinneyed in their stables, and even the flies upon the walls began to buzz. And on the staircase, the King and Queen arose as though their centuries of sleep had been but the doze of a summer afternoon.

Just then, the door above them opened and out stepped the young and handsome prince leading their lovely daughter by the arm.

"Here is the one who saved us all from harm", the princess said, "and he shall be my husband."

And so the princess and the prince were married, and so, just as the good, kind fairy said, the princess at last received the gift of happiness in love. They lived in joy for ever after, and would frequently tell their children and grandchildren how for three hundred years the princess slept, and how the good prince saved her with a kiss.

*THE LITTLE GIRL LAY BEFORE THE FIRE-
PLACE with her eyes closed. For a while, Willie thought that
she had fallen asleep and that the whole house, even the fire on
the hearth, the wind in the chimney, and the old clock below in
the kitchen was sleeping with her. But all at once, the clock
began to strike loudly, the fire began to crackle, the wind
whistled in the chimney and the little girl's eyes were open once
more, looking like green pools.*

"Another one!" she said.

*Willie only shook his head and snapped the book shut. He
didn't want to read any more, and anyway, he had never read
so much in his life before. Mother and Father would be surprised to see how he had improved! But he didn't mention this
to the little girl. He just waited without saying a word.*

*He didn't have to wait for long. Even though he was as
quiet as a mouse, she still put her finger to her lips for him to
be silent and listen to the still, quiet voice of the Wind in the
chimney telling the next story.*

FORTUNATUS
AND THE PRINCESS INIA DINIA

Once upon a time, long long ago, there lived a powerful emperor. He ruled over a huge empire and no other emperor in the whole world was as rich as he. In his imperial treasuries he had large barrels full of gold, silver and precious stones, and all of this wealth would one day fall to his only daughter, the young and beautiful Princess Inia Dinia.

Princess Inia Dinia was young and beautiful, and had everything she wanted, but in spite of this, she was sad and lonely. One day she came to her father and said, "O my Imperial Father, I have a great favour to ask of you. Would you build a little castle just for me at the other end of our garden?"

"With pleasure", replied the emperor, "but tell me, my daughter, with whom are you going to live there?"

"I shall tell you that", replied the Princess Inia Dinia, "when the castle is standing, O my Imperial Father."

And so the emperor had ten barrels of gold, ten barrels of silver, and ten barrels of precious stones rolled out of his treasuries, and then he called the best master builders and masons from all over his empire and the building began.

In a week, the castle was standing at the other end of the garden. Princess Inia Dinia was pleased. She went before her father and said, "O my Imperial Father, I thank you for the little castle. But now I have an even greater favour to ask of you. I would like you to have your empire searched for twelve maidens just as young and just as beautiful as I am. And then I shall live with them in my little castle."

"With pleasure," said the emperor, and he sent envoys into every corner of the empire to find twelve maidens just as young and just as beautiful as Princess Inia Dinia.

The envoys searched every corner of the empire and within a week they returned to the imperial castle with the maidens. But they only brought eleven.

"And where is the twelfth, O my Imperial Father?" asked Princess Inia Dinia.

"My envoys found the twelfth," replied the emperor, "but they could not bring her."

"And why not?" asked Princess Inia Dinia in surprise.

"Because she must look after her little brother," said the emperor. "His mother died the third day after he was born, and so the young and beautiful maiden must look after him."

"And in the whole empire can there be found no one else to care for the infant?" she asked. "Then bring them both, and we shall all look after the little one together."

And it was done as the Princess had asked. The envoys were sent to fetch the maiden, and the next day, they returned with her and her little brother. The Princess took an immediate liking to the little fellow.

"Just as I am called Inia Dinia," she said, "so this boy shall be called Fortunatus, which means 'The One Chosen by Fate'."

Then the Princess summoned the best nurse in the empire and turned little Fortunatus over into her care, saying, "Look after him, but in such a way that in one day he will grow as much as others in a month, and in one month as much as others in a whole year."

And the nurse replied, "It shall be as you have commanded, Princess!"

And truly, the nurse took such good care of little Fortunatus that every day he grew as much as others would have in a month, and every month as much as others in a whole year. When a year had gone by he was already a stalwart young lad, taller and more quick-witted than any other twelve-year-old. And then the Princess Inia Dinia decided that it was time to send Fortunatus to school. She had heard that in the capital city of the neighbouring empire there was the best school to be found anywhere, and so she made up her mind to send Fortunatus there.

She went before her father and said, "O my Imperial Father, I have a great favour to ask of you. I have heard that in the neighbouring empire there is the best school to be found anywhere, and I would like to send our Fortunatus there. He is so full of high spirits and so clever that he would most certainly profit from it. Could you take him there?"

"With pleasure," said the emperor, and the first thing the next morning he had six white horses hitched to his golden coach and prepared to make the long journey with Fortunatus.

But before they set off, Princess Inia Dinia took Fortunatus to one side and said to him, "Study well, my Destiny, and return to me soon. But remember one thing: no matter what happens, do not mention my name or anything about me to anyone. If you did, you would have to travel round the whole world before returning to us once more. Be very careful!"

"I shall, Princess," promised Fortunatus, the One Chosen by Fate, and he kissed the princess and jumped into the coach.

The emperor and Fortunatus travelled for a long, long time in their golden coach. They had to go over nine blue mountains, across nine blue lakes, and through nine blue forests before coming to the capital city of the neighbouring empire. There the emperor paid a courtesy visit to the ruler of that land and left Fortunatus to study at his famous school.

And in the very first lesson, Fortunatus gained the admiration of all his fellow pupils and teachers. "There has never yet been a student like him here," they all said in amazement. "If he goes on learning like this, he will one day become a very famous man."

Fortunatus attended the school for a whole year, and in that year he learned everything his teachers could teach him. And because there was nothing more to be learned, he decided to return home to Princess Inia Dinia and her twelve maidens. He appeared before the emperor and said, "O mighty Emperor, I have now learned everything there is to be learned in your school and so, with your grace, I should like to return home."

"If that is so, Fortunatus," replied the emperor, "then you may return, and God's blessing go with you. But first, drink with me for a safe journey."

"With pleasure," said Fortunatus, and he accepted the cup of wine offered him by the emperor's youngest son. He raised the cup to his lips and called out merrily, "Here's to the health of the mighty Emperor!"

And then he emptied the cup in one draught. The emperor was pleased with the toast. "Another one!" he ordered, and Fortunatus accepted a second cup of wine from the emperor's second son.

Lifting it to his lips, he called out merrily, "Here's to the health of the beautiful Empress!"

The emperor liked this toast even more. "For the third and last time," he commanded, and Fortunatus accepted a third cup of wine from the emperor's third and oldest son.

He lifted it to his lips, but because he was not used to wine, he forgot the Princess's warning and cried out gaily, "Here's to the health of the Princess Inia Dinia!"

This toast aroused the emperor's curiosity. "Who is this Princess Inia Dinia you speak of, Fortunatus?" he asked.

Fortunatus saw that he had made a mistake, but what could he do? No-one can take back a word once it is spoken. And so he said, "Princess Inia Dinia is the most beautiful and the wisest princess in the whole world. It was she who had me sent here to your school, and it was she who brought me up, and it was she who gave me the name Fortunatus, which means 'Chosen by Fate'."

And then the emperor frowned and said, "If this is so, Fortunatus, then you shall remain here with us until this Princess Inia Dinia comes to fetch you herself."

"But why, mighty emperor?" asked Fortunatus in bewilderment.

"Because I want to see with my own eyes if she is really as beautiful and wise as you say," said the emperor. "Until she comes, you are my prisoner."

"But how can she come if she doesn't know what has become of me?" pleaded Fortunatus.

"She will work it out for herself when you don't return for a long time," said the emperor, and then he called his guard.

From that time on, Fortunatus was the emperor's prisoner. True, he was not locked up in prison, and he could go wherever he wished in the emperor's palace and through the city, but he was not allowed to venture a single step beyond the city walls. And because he had nothing to do and nothing to work at, he soon found the time creeping by and he went about the palace like a body without a soul.

Meanwhile, the Emperor had begun to build a new palace. He summoned the best builders, master masons, stone-cutters and carpenters, and had stone, bricks and wood brought in and soon the city was resounding with the merry sounds of hammers pounding and saws sawing. Every day crowds of people gathered to watch the palace going up, and among them was good Fortunatus.

One day, one of the carpenters noticed him and said, "Tell me, Prince, why are you so unhappy all the time?"

And Fortunatus replied, "I am not a prince, master carpenter. I am an ordinary man like yourself and I am sad because I am homesick."

"And where is your home?" asked the carpenter.

"Beyond nine blue mountains, nine blue lakes and nine blue forests," sighed Fortunatus.

And the carpenter took pity on him and said, "If I could be of any help to you in your sorrow, I would do it gladly, from the bottom of my heart. But I do not know how."

"I know how you could help me", replied Fortunatus. "Make me a fine pipe to play on."

"Is that all?" said the master carpenter in surprise. "Nothing simpler! You shall have it in a week."

"And what can I give you in return?" asked Fortunatus.

"Nothing more than a jug of good wine with which I can drink your health," laughed the master carpenter.

"I shall even give you two," said Fortunatus, "if only you will make me a proper pipe."

And the carpenter made Fortunatus a pipe such as the world had never seen before. Of course, he worked very hard at it, carving away at it day and night for a week. But it was worth the effort, for when Fortunatus finally put the pipe to his lips and began to blow, it could be heard beyond nine blue mountains, nine blue lakes and nine blue forests.

"Thank you, master carpenter," cried Fortunatus happily. "And here are your two jugs of wine. Drink them to my health."

And he ran with his pipe to the highest tower in the emperor's palace. There, he placed it to his lips and began to play. He played softly, as if it were only for himself, but even that was enough. No sooner had he begun to play than the Princess Inia Dinia beyond the nine blue mountains and nine blue lakes and nine blue forests stopped her sewing by the open window of her palace.

"Listen, sisters!" she said to her twelve companions. "Do you hear that sad song? That can be no one else but my Fortunatus, Chosen by Fate. It is clear that because of me, they do not wish to let him return and now he is terribly homesick. Prepare for the journey; take your best clothes, and tomorrow morning we shall go for him."

The twelve beautiful maidens made ready for the long journey beyond nine blue mountains, nine blue lakes and nine blue forests. They locked the palace with twelve keys and stood in a row on the white marble staircase.

Then Princess Inia Dinia spoke to them. "Sisters, take each other by the hand and close your eyes."

The beautiful maidens closed their eyes, took each other by the hands, and together with Princess Inia Dinia they rose up into the air. They all flew in a row, one behind the other, like wild ducks flying south in the autumn. And a journey that would have taken a coach days and weeks, took them no time at all. Almost before they knew it they were standing before the palace where their beloved Fortunatus was being held prisoner.

The Princess appeared before the lord of the palace and said, "Why are you holding our Fortunatus, mighty Emperor?"

"Because he boasted of your beauty and wisdom, Princess Inia Dinia," replied the emperor. "I wanted you to come for him so that I could see for myself whether or not he was speaking the truth."

"Well, I have come, mighty Emperor, and you can satisfy yourself," she replied. "But first, give me our Fortunatus."

"Here he is now," said the emperor. "And I must say that he was speaking the truth. You may take him home with God's blessing."

But Inia Dinia did not take Fortunatus home with her. She led him aside and said to him firmly, "What have you done, Fortunatus? Did you disobey me and speak of me to anyone?"

"I did," Fortunatus admitted, and then he told her how it had happened.

"What's done is done," said Princess Inia Dinia.

"You have only made a lot of misery for yourself. If you wish to see me ever again, you must find me. I can no longer return home with my companions. You must buy yourself an iron staff and iron shoes and walk through the world with them until you have worn them through. Only then will you find me in a castle which is suspended from a golden hair and standing on a golden stalk."

When he heard this, Fortunatus began to weep bitterly. "I have waited for you so long, and now shall I have to wait for you again?" he cried.

"Do not weep," said Princess Inia Dinia comfortingly. "We cannot change what has happened. It had to happen. Even if you are chosen for me by Fate, you must still prove yourself worthy of me. When you find me, you shall never weep again. You will be happy with me as long as you live and your only wish will be that your happiness may never end."

And with that, Inia Dinia held out her hand to her twelve companions and they rose into the air like a flock of wild ducks flying south in the autumn. Before long, they had disappeared from sight.

And so poor Fortunatus was all alone once more. He went to the marketplace, bought himself an iron staff and iron shoes, put the shoes on his feet and set out to look for the castle suspended by a golden hair and standing on a golden stalk. But no one could tell him where that castle was, no matter who he asked and no matter where he went.

And so Fortunatus, the One Chosen by Fate, wandered across mountains and through valleys, across rivers and lakes, through woods and forests, and he walked all the way, the sooner to wear down his iron staff and to wear through his iron shoes.

As long as he had a few gold pieces in his purse, he lived on them, but when they were gone, he earned his livelihood by working. Once he worked as a stable boy, another time as a herdsman, and a third time he taught in one of the imperial schools. When he asked for a place as a school-master's assistant, they did not even believe that he could read and write. But when they began to ask him questions, they were even more astonished at how much he knew, and what he could do.

"Never yet have we had such an assistant here," they said. And they assigned him at once to teach the oldest boys. But Fortunatus was not able to accomplish much with them. The boys could not accept that a young man not much older than themselves was to teach them and test them, and they were so unruly and impolite, always making fun of his iron staff and iron shoes, that one night Fortunatus secretly set off once more to look for the castle suspended from the golden hair. When the school-master came the next morning to awaken his assistant, he found the bed empty.

The good Fortunatus, meanwhile, went on and on, over hill and dale, across mountains and valleys, rivers and seas, through woods and forests, until one day, on a wide, empty plain, he spied a very strange thing. Two creatures were locked in a life-and-death struggle, creatures such as Fortunatus had never seen before. At first he thought they were humans, but when he drew nearer, he saw that it was a dragoness and a demoness, and they were flailing and striking at each other so viciously that the sparks were flying.

When they saw a man approaching, they stopped fighting and said, "Judge our dispute, O wanderer, for we have been battling for three days and three nights now. Say which one of us is in the right, and we will abide by your decision."

"And why are you fighting?" asked Fortunatus, who was truly astonished.

"Because the dragoness brought a son into the world," replied the demoness, "and then she was too lazy to bring him up herself, and so she left him to fate. I took pity on the poor little fellow and so I took him in and looked after him until he was fourteen years old. And now that he is almost grown up, the dragoness suddenly wants him back again. Is that just?"

"No, it is not," replied Fortunatus. "The son belongs to the one who brought him up. It would be a fine thing if we could sit down to eat from a full table without working for it. The son is yours, demoness. And you, dragoness, you go your own way and leave the demoness in peace!"

"A thousand curses on both your heads," raged the dragoness, but there was nothing she could do, for she had agreed to abide by Fortunatus's decision.

But the demoness was delighted. "Thank you, wanderer, for your just decision. I hope that one day I shall be able to repay you."

And so each went off a different way, the dragoness in one direction, the demoness with her son in another, and good Fortunatus, as always, straight forwards to find the castle suspended on a golden hair. All at once he heard someone calling out to him, "Stop, wanderer, wait for me!"

Fortunatus turned around and whom did he see but the young boy raised by the demoness running after him.

When he had caught up, the young fellow said, "My mother sent me to go with you for a way. She says you might need me."

And so the two of them set off. Before long they came to a wide river. For as far as they could see in either direction there was neither a bridge nor a ford, but down by the riverbank, there was a ferryman's little boat bobbing up and down in the water.

"Can you take us across, ferryman?" said Fortunatus. "We'll be glad to pay you anything you ask."

"If you will pay anything I ask, then I shall be glad to take you across," replied the ferryman. "I hope you shall not regret it." And then he nodded Fortunatus and his companion into the boat.

But when they were almost across the river, the ferryman suddenly turned to them and said.

"And now, pay me! I demand one eye. And if you refuse, I shall drown the both of you on the spot!"

"An eye for a trip across the river?" cried Fortunatus. "Why that's unheard of!"

But his companion merely laughed. "Don't be afraid, Fortunatus. I'm here to help you."

And then he turned to the ferryman and said, "If you want an eye, come and get it!"

The ferryman pulled out a knife and jumped for the young fellow. But his evil was his own undoing, for no sooner had he touched the lad than he found himself flying through the air and into the water himself. Then Fortunatus and his companion landed safely on the other bank and went on their way.

After three days and three nights they came to a second river. It was even wider than the first and look as they might, they could see no bridge or ford anywhere. There was only a little boat belonging to a ferryman bobbing up and down by the bank.

"Take us across, ferryman," asked Fortunatus. "You shall receive anything you wish for it."

"If I may receive whatever I wish, then take you I shall," said the ferryman gruffly. "I only hope it won't seem too dear to you."

And he nodded for Fortunatus and his companion to jump into the boat.

When they were near the opposite bank, the ferryman suddenly turned to them and said, "And now pay me. I want one hand for the trip, otherwise I shall drown you both!"

"A hand for being taken across the river?" cried Fortunatus. "Why, that's unheard of!"

But his companion only laughed and said, "Don't be afraid, Fortunatus. I am here to protect you."

And then he turned to the ferryman and said, "If you want a hand, then come and get it!"

The ferryman took out his knife and jumped for the young fellow. But his own evil turned against him, for as soon as he touched the lad, he flew through the air and fell into the deep water himself. Then Fortunatus and his companion landed the boat safely on the other bank and went on their way.

In three days and three nights they came to a third river. It was bigger than both the others, and for as far as they could see in both directions there was neither a bridge nor a ford. There was only a little barque belonging to a ferryman bobbing up and down by the bank.

"Take us across the river," said Fortunatus, "and I will give you whatever you want."

"If you give me whatever I want," said the ferryman gruffly, "then I shall be glad to take you. But I don't want you complaining about the price afterwards." And he nodded for Fortunatus and his companion to get into the boat.

When they were nearing the other side, the ferryman suddenly turned to them and said, "And now you must pay me. I want a leg for it, otherwise I shall drown you both!"

"A leg for a trip across the river?" cried Fortunatus. "Why that's unheard of!"

But his companion only laughed and said, "There is nothing to be afraid of, Fortunatus. I am here to serve you."

And then he turned to the ferryman and said, "If you want a leg, then come and get it!"

The ferryman pulled out his knife and jumped for the young man. But his own evil turned against him, for as soon as he touched the lad, he flew through the air and into the depths of the river himself. Then Fortunatus and his friend landed safely on the other bank.

But there the demoness's son bade Fortunatus farewell. "You shall not need me any more, and so I shall return to my mother," he said. "But you must go on, and may luck go with you. You are not far from your destination now."

Fortunatus thanked his guide from the bottom of his heart, and then they parted. The demoness's son turned and hurried back the way they had come, and Fortunatus, his iron staff in his hand and the iron shoes on his feet, went on in search of the castle suspended from the golden hair.

He walked and walked and walked, until finally he had once more spent all his money and had to look for some kind of work. He found it with a miller. The miller had a mill by a swift-flowing river and he ground grain for the local farmers, and there was always enough work to be done.

When Fortunatus stopped at his mill one evening and asked if he could spend the night under his roof, the miller welcomed him warmly and said, "And where are you going, my lad?"

"God alone knows that," replied Fortunatus.

"And what are you looking for in this world?" asked the miller.

"Nothing more than a good master who will give me enough to eat and drink in return for an honest day's work," replied Fortunatus.

"Then stay with us," laughed the miller. "There is always plenty of work here, and bread too."

And so Fortunatus became a miller. Because he was clever, he learned the work very quickly and soon he was a better miller than his master. When the miller saw this, he gladly left all the work to Fortunatus and went about doing whatever he pleased. He would go into the woods to hunt, or to the market in the town, and who knows where else.

There was an old man who used to bring grain to be ground every month. He would come with a sack of grain slung over his horse's back, and each time he would wait until the grain was ground. But no one knew who he was or where he came from.

One day, the old man came to the mill when Fortunatus was there alone. Fortunatus ground the grain while he waited, and he did it so well that the old man was astonished, for he had never seen such fine flour in his life.

But even more surprised was his mistress, who lived in a castle suspended on a golden hair and standing on a golden stalk.

"Who ground this beautiful flour?" she asked the old man.

"The miller's new helper," he replied.

"In that case, give him this ducat from me the next time you go," said the mistress of the castle, "for I have never seen such fine flour in all my life."

And when, a month later, the old man took the grain to the mill to be ground, he gave Fortunatus the golden ducat as his mistress had instructed.

"Our mistress sends you this for grinding our grain so finely," he said.

Fortunatus was pleased with the gift and the honour, and properly so, but the miller's wife flew into a rage. As soon as the miller came home, she began to shout at him. "Fortunatus got a gold ducat from the old man for grinding the grain and you get nothing, though you've been grinding his grain all these years! We are losing money because of that vagabond. Get rid of him at once, or we shall end up in the poor-house!"

The old miller tried to defend Fortunatus, but the miller's wife kept at him so long that she finally persuaded him. The miller took Fortunatus to one side and told him, "There's nothing to be done about it, my boy. My wife wants me to let you go, and so you had better leave, and God be with you."

"I shall go," replied Fortunatus. "Anyway, I shall never find peace in this world until I wear down this iron staff of mine and wear out these iron shoes."

He thanked the miller for giving him work and bread and then he set out into the world once more.

On the way, he caught up with the old man with the sack of flour. "And where are you off to, young man?" he asked Fortunatus.

"Into the world, old man," replied Fortunatus. "They no longer have any work for me at the mill. There wouldn't be any work for me where you come from, would there?"

"I can't say," replied the old man, shaking his head. "First I would have to ask our mistress, Princess Inia Dinia."

Good Fortunatus could hardly believe his own ears. If he had heard aright, then his wanderings were almost at an end. But he mentioned not a word of this to the old man. He went along with him until the Princess's castle appeared before them. And truly, it was suspended on a golden hair and standing on a golden stalk, and whenever a breeze blew, it swayed gently in the air like a huge golden ship on the sea. A high ladder led to it from the ground.

Just before they came to the ladder, Fortunatus parted with the old man. He stopped at a nearby inn and there he dressed himself as a painter. And when this was done, he plucked up his courage and climbed the ladder to the castle.

In the courtyard, he began to call out, "New colours for old! New colours for old! With my paint and my brush I give new rooms for old!"

And no sooner had he begun to shout this than a window above his head flew open and one of the Princess's twelve beautiful companions waved at him and said, "Hey there, painter! Come up here. My room needs painting."

"I'll be there in a flash", cried Fortunatus gaily, and up the stairs he flew.

The maiden was waiting for him and she took him into her room. Fortunatus wasted no time in setting to work and in half a day the room was painted, but so beautifully that the maiden could only stare and clasp hands in delight.

"What can I give you for such work?" she asked.

"Nothing, fair maiden," replied Fortunatus. "A kind word and a piece of bread is enough."

Meanwhile a second maid came running up and when she saw the beautiful work which the merry painter had done, she asked him to paint her room too. Fortunatus was very glad to oblige her. He set to work painting the second room, and then a third and then a fourth, until he had painted the rooms of all twelve of Princess Inia Dinia's companions.

Just as he was finishing the twelfth room, the princess herself came to see him. She was so impressed by the work of this unknown painter that she wanted to have her chamber painted too. And so she said.

"Would you paint my room as well, good fellow?"

"With pleasure, fair Princess," replied Fortunatus, and he set to work immediately.

This time he took special care, and when he finished, the Princess was filled with wonder and admiration.

"And what can I give you for such beautiful work?" she asked.

"Nothing more than a kind word and a slice of bread," said Fortunatus, throwing off his painter's cap and coat.

And then the Princess recognized who it was standing before her. "So you have come at last, my Fortunatus!" she cried joyfully. "You have finally found me!"

"I have found you, Princess Inia Dinia," said Fortunatus, "and if you do not turn me out, I shall stay with you forever."

"How could I possibly turn you out when I have been waiting for you all this time," she said, kissing Fortunatus on both cheeks. "How could I possibly turn you out, when you are my Chosen One."

And she called all her twelve companions together and said.

"Our Fortunatus has returned, and because he has worn down his iron staff and worn through his iron shoes for me, he has proved that he deserves my heart and hand. Go and prepare a wedding the like of which the world has never yet seen."

And so the good Fortunatus, Chosen by Fate, married the Princess Inia Dinia, and ever since then they have been living happily together in eternal youth, because in the castle suspended on the golden hair and standing on the golden stalk, no one ever grows old and no one ever dies.

WILLIE DID NOT HAVE THE SLIGHTEST IDEA
how it was that he woke up every morning in his bed. All he remembered was listening to those stories with the little girl by the fireside, but what happened after that, and how he got under the warm eiderdown, he simply could not remember. Nor did he know when the little girl went away, or how she went.

One morning he decided to investigate. He jumped out of bed and ran straight to the cold fireplace, but he didn't discover very much. He did get very dirty however, and Granny saw immediately what he had done.

"Willie!" she shouted at him. "What were you doing in the fireplace?"

Willie had to think of an excuse quickly. "I was trying to see if it's true that you can see the stars through the chimney even in the daytime," he said.

Granny had to laugh at his excuse. "I had no idea you wanted to be an astronomer!" she said, and then she added severely, "Once more, young fellow, and you'll sleep in the kitchen!"

Willie didn't want that. And so the whole day he did his best to be good, until finally Granny forgot that she was angry with him. She even gave him a handful of peanuts after supper.

The little girl liked the peanuts very much. They began to shell them together as soon as they met on the bear-skin rug in front of the fireplace. And so that Granny would't be annoyed at the mess, they threw the shells into the fire. The fiery little men were delighted, and began to dance.

They danced so long and Willie and the little girl were so fascinated that they very nearly forgot all about the fairy-tales. But when they had finished eating the peanuts and the fiery little men had finished dancing, it was finally time for a story. Willie opened his book and began to read very slowly and carefully. And this is what he read.

THE TABLE, THE DONKEY, AND THE STICK IN THE SACK

Once upon a time there was a tailor who had three sons. The first and the oldest had hair as black as coal and so they called him Blackhead. The middle son had hair the colour of bricks, and so they called him Redhead. And the youngest had hair as yellow as ripe wheat, and so they called him Goldenhead. Otherwise, all three brothers were equally sturdy, equally well-mannered, and equally hardworking, and when they grew up, they were all fine young men and very clever craftsmen. Blackhead learned carpentry, Redhead became a cooper, and Goldenhead was a baker.

But in the poor village where they lived, there was little chance for them to make their fortune, so the boys decided to go into the world. Blackhead was the first to ask his father.

"Father," he said, "let me go into the world. Perhaps my fortune is waiting for me there."

His father agreed. "Of course, my boy", he said. "Go, and may you fare well and return safely!"

And so Blackhead took leave of his parents, said farewell to his brothers, and set out into the world to seek his fortune.

He searched a long, long time, walking wherever his legs would take him, until he had spent everything his father had given him, and still he had not found his fortune, nor even a bit of honest work. Once, when he was sitting sadly by the side of the road thinking over his troubles, he heard someone call out to him, "I say there, young fellow, what are you looking so sad about?"

Blackhead looked up and saw standing before him a kind old man with long white hair and a beard that reached the ground.

"I'm going into the world, old man," replied Blackhead. "I set out to seek my fortune, but so far I've not even come across any honest work."

"And what can you do?" asked the old man.

"I'm a carpenter," replied Blackhead.

"Just what I'm looking for!" said the old man delightedly. "Come with me and you'll not regret it. If you serve me well, you shall be well rewarded for it!"

Blackhead did not need to be persuaded. He picked up his bundle and set off after the old man. Before long they were standing in front of a nice little cottage where a kind old woman was greeting them from the doorway.

"Come along now, dinner is waiting," she called.

The old man led Blackhead inside, sat him down at the table, and poured him a big bowl of soup. After they had eaten, he took the young man around the cottage and showed him what had to be done and what to repair. Blackhead set to work eagerly and before the week was out, everything was finished and the cottage shone like new. The old man was very satisfied.

"I see, Blackhead, that you are a fine lad and a good craftsman. You have worked well and I would like to reward you well for it. I have no money, but I shall give you something even better."

And he took Blackhead into a little room which was always locked and took out a small table.

"This table is yours," he said. "It looks just like any other, but don't be mistaken. This is a magic table. If you say, 'Table, spread yourself', in the twinkling of an eye it will be spread with whatever you want to eat. Make the most of it, but be careful not to let anyone take it from you."

Blackhead could hardly believe his ears. He threw the little table over his shoulders, thanked the old man and his wife, bade them farewell, and then hurried homewards.

The way home was long, and when it was about midday, Blackhead became very hungry. He sat down in the shade of a grove by the side of the road, set the table on the ground in front of him and suddenly he thought, "Why don't I try the table?"

And without another moment's delay, he commanded, "Table, spread yourself!"

The old man's table was truly magic. In the twinkling of an eye, the table was covered with a white cloth and on the cloth was a loaf of bread, a plate of roast meat and a bottle of good wine. Blackhead ate and drank his fill and then merrily went on his way, the little table on his shoulders.

Late that evening, he came to a village and asked for lodging at an inn.

"We have beds enough," said the innkeeper gruffly, "but there is no more food. My guests have eaten everything."

"Don't worry," said Blackhead. "I have food enough for everyone."

And with that, he set the old man's table in the middle of the room and commanded, "Table, spread yourself!"

And in the twinkling of an eye, the table was spread with a feast for every guest in the inn.

Eyeing all this enviously, the innkeeper said to himself, "A table like that is just what I need, for the money would come rolling in and I wouldn't have to lift a finger."

And when Blackhead had eaten his fill, the innkeeper gave him his best room and then waited until he was sound asleep. Then he found a little table that looked just like the magic one and he crept into Blackhead's room to exchange them.

When Blackhead woke up next morning, he was none the wiser. The innkeeper gave him breakfast in bed, so there was no need for him to use his table. Blackhead ate a hearty meal, bade farewell to the innkeeper, and then hurried home with the table over his shoulders.

His homecoming was truly a surprise. His mother and father wept for joy when they saw him and his brothers gathered round and asked inquisitively, "Well, Blackhead, what is it like in the world? Did you find your fortune?"

"I did," replied Blackhead proudly, "and here it is — this little table."

"Just a common table?" they all exclaimed in astonishment.

"This is no ordinary table," replied Blackhead. "It's a magic table, and it will give us a feast for the whole village. Just invite all the neighbours over and I'll show you."

His father shook his head at all this, but his brothers hurried out and invited the neighbours to the feast. Soon their house was full, and Blackhead placed the little table in the middle of the room and said "Table, spread yourself!"

But nothing happened, and plead, order, and threaten as he might, Blackhead could not persuade the table to spread itself. The neighbours laughed at him and poor Blackhead wept bitter tears and said, "That innkeeper must have exchanged my magic table for this one."

But his tears were of no avail and so Blackhead once more had to take up his trade as a carpenter. And the second brother, Redhead, set out into the world.

He too searched his long, long time for a fortune, but nowhere could he find it. And once, when he was sitting thinking about his ill luck by the side of the road, he heard a voice calling, "I say there young fellow, why are you hanging your head so?"

Redhead looked up and saw the same old man standing before him that his brother had seen some time ago.

"I have set out into the world to seek my fortune, old man," replied Redhead, "but I have had no luck at all, and I haven't even been able to find a bit of decent work. I'm a cooper by trade."

"Just what I'm looking for," said the man delightedly. "Come with me, and if you serve me well, you shall be well rewarded for it."

The old man took Redhead to his little cottage and after giving him a good meal, he showed him an empty cellar, saying he needed some barrels made. Redhead set to work eagerly, and before the week was out, his work was finished.

The old man was pleased. "I see, Redhead, that you are a fine lad and a good craftsman. You have worked well and I shall reward you well for it."

And he took Redhead into his stable and showed him a handsome donkey. "This donkey is yours," he said. "It looks just like any other, but don't be mistaken, for this is a magic donkey. If you say, 'Shake, donkey, shake,' to it, in the twinkling of an eye gold pieces will pour from it. Make the most of it, but be very careful."

Redhead could hardly believe his ears. He took the donkey by the bridle, thanked the old man and his wife politely, said his farewells, and then hurried homewards.

The way was long, and finally he arrived at the inn where his brother Blackhead had once spent the night. When he asked for supper and a bed, the inkeeper replied gruffly, "There will be supper and a bed if you can pay for them."

"Of course I can," laughed Redhead. "I have as much money as you want."

And with no further ado, he stood his donkey in the middle of the yard and commanded, "Shake, donkey, shake!"

The donkey shook and in the twinkling of an eye the ground around it was scattered with gold pieces just waiting to be picked up.

The innkeeper eyed all this enviously, and said to himself, "A donkey like that is just what I need, for I would be rich till the end of my days."

And when Redhead had eaten his fill, the innkeeper gave him the best room and waited until he was sound asleep. Then he ran to the stable, led Redhead's donkey away and tied his own, which looked just like it, in its place.

In the morning, Redhead was none the wiser. He had a good breakfast, bade farewell to the inkeeper, and hurried home, leading the donkey on a rope.

At home, they all wept for joy to see him again, and his brothers gathered round and asked him inquisitively whether he had found luck and fortune in the world.

"I have," replied Redhead proudly. "And here it is — this donkey."

"But that's just an ordinary donkey," they all said in surprise.

"No, it's not," replied Redhead. "It's a magic donkey. When it shakes, there will be enough money for everyone in the village, and some left over. Just invite over the neighbours and I'll show you."

His brothers invited over all the neighbours and soon the whole yard was full. Then Redhead led his donkey into the middle of the yard and commanded, "Shake, donkey, shake!"

But nothing happened. The donkey did not shake, and gold coins did not fall from it, no matter how much Redhead pleaded with it and threatened it. All the neighbours laughed and poor Redhead wept angry tears and said, "That innkeeper must have exchanged my magic donkey for this one."

And so there was nothing for him to do but take up his cooper's trade once more, and the third brother Goldenhead set out into the world.

He walked through the world for a long time, looking for luck and fortune, and finally his path too crossed with the old man's. He was sitting by the side of the road trying to think what to do next, when all at once he heard someone calling out to him, "I say there, young fellow, why are you sitting there so sadly?"

Goldenhead looked up and saw the old man with white hair and a white beard that reached down to the ground standing before him.

"I have set out into the world to seek my fortune, old man," answered Goldenhead, "but I have had no luck so far, not even an honest bit of work. I'm a baker by trade."

"That's just what I'm looking for," said the old man delightedly. "Come with me, and if you serve me well, then I shall reward you well for it."

And so Goldenhead too came to the little cottage where the old man lived with his wife. Before the week was out, he had baked them so many loaves of bread and so many buns and muffins that the old couple had enough left over to sell. The old man was very pleased. "I see, Goldenhead, that you are a a fine lad and an excellent baker," he said. "You have worked well and now I shall reward you well for it. Here is a sack. It looks like any other, but don't be mistaken, for it is a magic sack. When you say 'Stick, out of the sack!' a stick will fly out and beat your enemies until they can no longer stand up. And when you cry 'Stick, enough!' the stick jumps back into the sack again. Make the most of it and luck will come your way, you'll see."

Goldenhead could hardly believe his ears. He threw the sack over his shoulder, thanked the old couple politely, then bade them farewell and hurried homewards.

"And I know," he said merrily to himself, "where that luck is awaiting me."

The way home was long and Goldenhead was glad when he finally arrived at the inn where his brothers had stayed. When he asked the innkeeper for supper and a bed, the man replied gruffly, "You shall have supper and a bed but only if you can pay for them."

"That I can," laughed Goldenhead. "My sack there will pay for me. Keep it for me until morning. It has magic powers, but you mustn't say to it 'Stick, out of the sack' or there will be trouble."

The innkeper said to himself as he took the sack, "I wonder what could be in it? I must try it and see."

And then he gave Goldenhead a good supper and afterwards put him in the best room in the inn and then waited until he was asleep. Then he took out the magic sack and said impatiently, "Stick, out of the sack!"

The stick didn't wait to be asked twice. It jumped out of the sack and began to beat the innkeeper so soundly that the dust flew. The innkeeper shouted, he wailed, he pleaded and he begged, but all in vain. The stick would not be stopped.

The innkeeper's cries woke Goldenhead. He ran into the room and said, "So that is how you treat a stranger's things, innkeeper. Stick, go to him, and don't let up until he returns my brother's table!"

The innkeeper writhed and shrieked with pain, but finally he gave in. "It's over there in the closet. Take it, but please stop this stick!"

Goldenhead found his brother's table in the closet, but he didn't stop the stick. "Just keep on, stick, for it isn't everything. Don't let up until he returns my brother's donkey as well!"

The innkeeper writhed and shrieked with pain, but he finally gave in. "It's over there in the stable. Take it, but please stop this stick!"

Goldenhead found the donkey in the stable, and then he called out, "Enough, stick!"

The stick jumped back into the sack and the innkeeper fetched a sigh of relief. But he kept on wailing and sighing for a long time as he watched Goldenhead going homewards with the little table, the donkey and the sack with the stick.

At home, they wept with joy to see him and his brothers gathered round and asked him curiously, "Well, Goldenhead, did you find any luck in the world?"

"I did," laughed Goldenhead. "And here it is — this table, this donkey and this sack with the stick."

"But that is my table!" cried Blackhead joyously.

"And that is my donkey!" cried Redhead happily.

"And so they are," said Goldenhead. "But it was my stick and my sack that got them back from the innkeeper for you."

And then he showed his brothers what the sack could do.

The brothers were not really angry at receiving a few blows from the stick. They were glad to have their magic gifts back, and all of them lived happily and merrily ever after. The table provided them with food, the donkey with pieces of gold, and the sack kept a faithful watch over all.

ONCE AGAIN, THE TALE WAS OVER. The little girl had three little figures in her hand. Once of them had hair as black as a raven and was carrying a little table on his back. The second had hair like fire and he was leading a donkey on a rope. And the third had hair like the sun and he had a stick in his hand. And all three of them danced, even with the table, the donkey and the stick, until the little girl blew at them and they disappeared like the flame of a candle when you blow it out.

Willie snapped the book shut to let her know that he had already read enough.

The little girl laughed. "All right," she said, "let's listen."

And she put her finger to her lips for him to be quiet, and from the chimney came the still, quiet voice of the Wind telling this story.

THE PRINCESS
AND THE GREEN KNIGHT

Once upon a time, long ago, there was a King who ruled happily over his kingdom with his dear wife and only daughter. But his happiness was short-lived, for one day the Queen was taken abed and before the week was out, she was on the very edge of death. In her last hours, she called the King to her bedside and said, "My lord, I know that my end is near, and so I have one last request to make of you. Promise me that you will never deny our daughter anything she asks for."

With tears in his eyes, the King promised, and shortly after that the dear Queen passed away. For one long year the old King and his daughter mourned her, and they might still be mourning today had they not received a visit from a certain noble lady from a near-by castle. She was a widow who lived alone with her daughter, and when she heard of the King's grief, she came to share his sorrow with him.

The King was not very happy with his uninvited guest, but the little princess was delighted. The noble lady looked after her, her daughter played with her all day long, and both of them agreed what a fine thing it would be if they could stay with the princess for ever.

134

"And why couldn't you?" asked the princess in surprise.

"Because we are only here for a visit," said the noble lady. "Unless you ask your father the King to marry me. Then we could stay with you forever and you would have a new mother and a sister."

The princess was soon persuaded. She longed to have a mother and a sister and so she went to her father and pleaded with him to marry the noble lady.

At first, the King would not even hear of the idea. "You don't know what you are asking, girl!" he said sternly. "You would certainly regret it."

But the princess insisted. "I won't regret it, Father. Do it for me."

And so the old King finally did get married. He kept the promise which he had made to his poor wife and did what his dear daughter had asked him to, but very soon he regretted it. And the princess regretted it even more. The wedding was scarcely over when the noble lady changed and so did her daughter. They no longer looked after the little princess, they no longer played with her and talked with her the whole day as before. Quite the contrary, whenever they could, they scolded her, whenever they met her, they did some wrong to her, and most of all they would like to have driven her out of the royal castle altogether.

All this made the poor princess very unhappy and for days on end she went about with her eyes red from crying. Finally she went to her father the King and complained. But what could the King do?

"I told you that you would regret it," he told the princess sadly. "But it's too late to do anything about it now. It would be best to get out of their sight. Go and live for a while in our summer residence. You will feel better there."

The King was right. The summer residence was on an island far out in the sea and the princess lived there for a long time in peace with her small court of several servants and maidservants.

But while the princess was living in peace on her island, her father the King was beset by great difficulties. A neighbouring kingdom was preparing war against him and one day the war really broke out. And so the King had to go to battle, but before setting off, he went to see his daughter.

"I must go to war," he said, "and so I have come to say farewell and to ask what you would like me to bring you from the campaign."

"You needn't bring me anything, Father," replied his daughter, "I only want you to come back to me soon and in good health. But if you still want to do something for me, then give my greetings to the Green Knight."

The old King was surprised, for he had never heard of any Green Knight. But if he was surprised, the princess was even more so, for neither had she. She had just blurted it out without even knowing why herself. "Very well," the King promised. "If I find this Green Knight, I shall give him your greetings." And then he bade farewell to the princess and was gone.

His campaign was long and hard, but it ended in victory. The King defeated his enemies and he was preparing to return when all at once he remembered his promise. But where and how to begin looking for this green Knight he truly did not know. And so, accompanied by his men, he roamed from country to country, from kingdom to kingdom, but wherever he asked about the Green Knight, he was always told that no one had ever heard of him at all.

It wasn't until he was almost at the end of the world that someone told him about a land where everything was green, not only the trees and the grass, but the houses and the castles as well. In short, everything was green. "And that," he was told, "is where your Green Knight lives."

And so the King set off with his company to find this green land. Finally, after a long journey, he stood in the courtyard of a beautiful green castle, and on the green staircase before the green gate of that green castle stood the Green Knight himself dressed in beautiful green clothes.

"Welcome, noble sir," said the Green Knight, "and tell me what brings you to me."

"I bring you greetings from my daughter," replied the King.

But the Green Knight was not content with this reply, for he wanted to know more about the princess who had sent him the greetings. He invited the King and his company into his green castle and there he gave them a royal feast. After the banquet was over, the Green Knight asked the King, "Tell me, noble sir, who is your daughter and where does she live?"

And the King told the Green Knight just how it all was, that his daughter lived on an island in the sea and that she had asked him to give her greetings to the Green Knight, although no one at home had ever heard of him.

The Green Knight shook his head when he heard this, and next day, when the King was preparing to leave, he brought him a green book and asked him to give it to the princess as a gift.

"Let her read this book whenever she is unhappy," said the Green Knight. "But before she opens it, let her first open the window and call out three times:

"Let all things round me slumber,
Let all things round me sleep,
That I may read and ponder
In concentration deep."

The King thanked the Green Knight for the gift and promised to give it to his daughter. And then he set out for home. When he arrived, the first thing he did was to visit his beloved daughter to give her the Green Knight's present and his message.

The princess was overjoyed with the book. And because that very evening a strange sadness suddenly came over her, she tried its powers out at once. As soon as it was dark, she sent all her maidservants to bed, opened the window and called out three times:

"Let all things round me slumber,
Let all things round me sleep,
That I may read and ponder
In concentration deep."

She had scarcely finished saying it for the third time when the whole household and everything around it fell into a deep sleep. Only the princess in the open window remained awake. She sat on the sill turning the pages of the green book. But not for long, however, for all at once she heard a rustling outside and in through the window, on large green wings, flew the Green Knight himself.

The princess was frightened, and well she might have been. "Who are you, strange sir?" she asked.

"I am the one to whom you sent your greetings, princess," replied the Green Knight. "I wanted to see you with my own eyes. I wanted to talk with you, and bring you a gift from my own land."

And he gave the princess a ring with a huge green stone in it. The princess liked the ring very much, but she liked the Green Knight even more. They talked together the whole night long, and it wasn't until the first pink light of dawn began to appear over the sea that the Green Knight said farewell to the princess, spread his greeen wings and flew away.

The princess thought about him the whole day, but after her supper, she felt so sad again that she had to try out the power of the book for a second time. As soon as it was dark, she sent all her servants to bed and called out three times through the open window:

"Let all things round me slumber,
Let all things round me sleep,
That I may read and ponder
In concentration deep."

She had scarcely finished saying it for the third time when a deep sleep fell upon the house and everything around it. Only the princess at the open window did not sleep. She turned the pages of the green book and thought about the Green Knight. But before she could get very far in her thoughts, something rustled outside the window and once more the Green Knight himself flew in.

This time he brought the princess a gift of earrings set with magnificent green stones. The princess liked the earrings very much but she liked the Green Knight himself even more. Once again, they talked until dawn.

But while the princess was talking all night with the Green Knight, her step-mother was consulting with her spies. For a long time now it had been a thorn in her flesh that her step-daughter was living like a Queen on her island in the sea, and now she had heard that every day, the princess received new jewels, first a golden ring with a green stone, then earrings with green stones, and who could say what next?

"There is more to this than meets the eye," she said, and the very next day she set out to visit the princess on her island. She arrived in great pomp and the first thing she noticed at the welcoming was the princess's new jewels. As soon as she found a suitable moment, she asked one of the servants about them.

"Where did the princess get those new jewels?" she snapped. "Does anyone come to visit her?"

"She has no visitors," replied the servants as truthfully as they knew how. "We have seen no one, and we know of no one. All we know is that the princess sits in her open window every evening reading the green book which her father the King brought back with him."

"In her open window?" said the evil Queen in astonishment. So she waited until evening when the princess had gone into the garden, and then she slipped into her room and pounded six long, sharp nails covered with poison into the window-frame.

The princess knew nothing of all this. As soon as it was dark, she sent her servants to bed, opened the window and called out three times:

"Let all things round me slumber,
Let all things round me sleep,
That I may read and ponder
In concentration deep."

No sooner had she finished saying the words when a deep sleep fell on everything and before long, the rustling of great wings sounded outside and the Green Knight flew in through the window. But instead of greeting the princess gaily as usual, he moaned, "Ah, what have you done to me, princess! Why have you betrayed me. Why did you set those big, sharp poisonous nails in the window to trap me?"

And before the princess could say a word in her own defense, before she could help him, he had flown once more into the darkness on heavy wings. He never appeared at the princess's window again, and the princess never again called him with her green book. And how could she have, when the Green Knight himself lay in his own green palace, dying of the deep wounds which covered his body. Though doctors from all over the world came to his bedside, none could help him, none could find the proper cure.

Rumours about the Green Knight's illness flew round the world and in time they reached the ears of the dear princess. When she heard of how the Green Knight was suffering, when she heard that he was dying and that there was no cure and no help for him, she secretly gathered together her jewels and her clothes, tied them into a bundle, put on a simple smock and set out into the world.

Across mountains, through valleys, over rivers and through woods, she walked courageously on until at long last the towers of the green castle rose out of the woods ahead. The princess was overjoyed, but at the same time her heart was sore with worry. She had reached her destination, but she had no cure for the Green Knight, nor did she have any idea how to help him. At the mere thought of her own helplessness her eyes ran with tears. And she wept so hard that she did not notice an old white-haired man standing before her.

"Why what's the matter with you, little girl, that you are crying so?" asked the old man in a kindly voice.

"What's the matter with me, old man?" replied the princess. "I am unhappy because I have no cure for my best beloved."

And she told the old man who she was and why she had come so far. And when the old man had heard her story, he began to cheer her up.

"Why if it is nothig worse than that," he said, "then I shall help you. There, under that tree, there is a rock, and under the rock a mother snake has a nest with nine little snakes. If you take those little snakes and make three meals of them for the Green Knight, he will surely recover. His wounds are full of poison and only poison can cure him, you can believe me."

The princess believed the old man. She thanked him for his advice and did what he had told her. She took the nine little snakes from the nest, wrapped them in her kerchief and walked on to the green castle. When she arrived, she asked if they had any work for her.

"Indeed we do," replied the castellan. "Go and help the washerwomen over there. For three weeks now they have been trying to wash the blood from our master's shirt, but it is still just as blood-stained as when he returned that night with wounds all over his body."

The princess did not wait to be asked twice. She rolled up her sleeves, took the shirt and lo! when she dipped it in the water, the blood began to run of it. She dipped it in a second time, and almost all the blood had disappeared, and when she dipped it in the water and drew it out for the third time, the shirt was as white as fresh snow. And at the very same moment, like a miracle, all the Green Knight's wounds closed.

Although the Green Knight's wounds had miraculously healed, he was still not well. He could not get out of bed, nor could he eat. When the princess heard this, she asked the cook to let her prepare something for the Knight with her own hands.

"Indeed you can," replied the cook. "Go over there to the kitchen and help my assistants. Anyway, they have been cooking for three weeks and they can't seem to prepare anything that our master will eat."

The princess did not wait to be asked twice. She rolled up her sleeves, took three little snakes out of her kerchief, and cooked a supper of them for the Knight. When they took it to him, he ate it all right down to the last mouthful and immediately felt better. The same evening, he called his cook to him and ordered him to prepare the same dish again tomorrow.

"I didn't cook your supper, my lord. It was our new servant girl," said the cook, and he ran to the princess and asked her if she would prepare the same meal for the Knight again.

The princess did not wait to be asked twice. She took another three little snakes from her kerchief and made such a dish that when the Green Knight had eaten it, he could sit up in bed.

"If I could just have one more meal like that one," he said to his chief cook, "I could get out of bed and I would be completely well again."

The chief cook ran to ask the princess to cook her miraculous meal once more and for the last time.

The princess did as she was told gladly. She took the last three little snakes and made such a dish that when the Green Knight had eaten it, he jumped out of bed and was completely well again.

"And now I would like to see the maid who prepared those three suppers for me," he said to his cook. "Send her to my room in the morning."

In the morning the chief cook called the princess and said to her, "Here is a jug of water. Take it to our master."

There was nothing for the princess to do but obey, but when she entered the Green Knight's chamber with the jug, she turned around and ran out again so quickly that the Knight scarcely had a chance to look at her.

"Send her to me again tomorrow morning," he commanded the chief cook. "She ran in and out again so quickly that I could scarcely get a good look at her."

The next day the cook called the princess and said, "Here is a duster. Take it to our master."

There was nothing for the princess to do but obey, but when she had entered the Green Knight's chamber with the duster, she turned around and ran out again so quickly that the Knight scarcely had a chance to see her face.

"Tomorrow send her to me once more," he commanded the chief cook. "She ran in and out again so quickly that I didn't even have a chance to see her face."

And so the third day, the cook called the princess once more and said to her, "Here is a mirror and a comb. Take it to our master."

There was nothing for the princess to do but obey, but when she entered the Green Knight's chamber with the mirror and comb, she couldn't turn around and run out again as quickly as before, because she was afraid of breaking the mirror or dropping the comb. And so the Green Knight had a chance to stop her from leaving so quickly. He took her by the hand, looked into her face, and said, "Was it you who washed my shirt?"

"Yes, it was me," nodded the princess.

"And was it you who cooked me those three meals?" he asked again.

"Yes, that was me as well," nodded the princess.

The Green Knight asked one more question. "And are you the beautiful princess from the island?"

And a third time the princess nodded, "Yes, I am."

And so the Green Knight met his beloved princess again, and the dear princess had found and saved her Green Knight. They talked together all day and all night until dawn, and when they had said all there was to say and kissed until they could kiss no more, they set off to see the princess's father.

And there in the old King's castle they held a glorious wedding and they ate and drank and enjoyed each other's company together for a whole ten days. Everyone at the wedding was happy and gay, except for the evil Queen, whose heart nearly burst from envy and wrath. But the Green Knight and his princess had room in their hearts only for rejoicing, and when the wedding was over, they returned to their green land and there they lived in happiness and contentment for ever after.

NEXT MORNING, THE POSTMAN BROUGHT A LETTER from Mother and Father. They asked how Willie was. Granny smiled and said, "Well, Willie, what shall we tell them?"

Willie was on tenterhooks. He didn't really know what to say. But Grannie had an answer. "We'll tell them not to worry about a thing. And that they should come on Saturday or Sunday."

Willie was satisfied. He was looking forward to seeing his Mother and Father, but at the same time he didn't want his evenings by the fireplace to come to an end. And so he only nodded eagerly while Granny wrote the reply, and then willingly he ran to meet the postman with the letter. He would mail it for them. He wouldn't forget.

That evening Willie rushed through his supper and then asked to go straight to bed. Granny was somewhat surprised at his haste, but she said nothing. As soon as she closed the door behind her, Willie hurried to the fireplace, but it was still too early, for the little girl was not there. So Willie sat gazing into the fire until his eyelids began to droop. He must have dropped off to sleep for a while, because he dreamt that a long arm reached down the chimney holding the little girl in the palm of its hand. She jumped out of the hand, walked through the fire to Willie and the arm disappeared. When Willie opened his eyes, the little girl was already sitting on the bear's head.

First they played for a while, then the little girl made her figurines and animals and Willie caught them, until his hands were all covered with ash. And when they had quite enough, the little girl snuggled into her favourite place on the bear's head and there was nothing for Willie to do but open the book. Slowly, and very carefully, he began to read, and this is what he read.

BEAUTY AND THE BEAST

Once upon a time there was a wealthy merchant who had three daughters, each one prettier than the next. All three were pretty, as I say, but the youngest was the prettiest and she was also the most kind-hearted. And that is why no one ever called her anything but Beauty, and the name stayed with her. Both her older sisters envied her, and what they lacked in beauty and kindness, they made up for in pride and fine clothing. They carried themselves about as haughtily as two princesses and for a long time they really believed that some day two princes would come and take them away. But no prince came, for one day, the merchant's fortunes took a sudden turn. His trade began to fail,

144

he lost several ships at sea with all their cargoes, and finally he was forced to sell his fine house in the city and move to the country.

The older sisters were very unhappy, for suddenly they found themselves living in a poor country cottage far from their friends and would-be suitors. But Beauty was not distressed, for she was much happier in the country than in the city. She looked after the house, did the cooking and cleaning, tended the flower garden, and was glad that she could be of some help to her father.

All this went against the older sisters' nature. "Just look at our little Beauty," they would say scornfully. "Why she even enjoys her misfortune! She is so content here in the country that she clearly deserves nothing better. But why should we have to suffer so?"

But their suffering was not so great as they imagined. They got up every day at noon, and then spent half a day preening themselves before the mirror. Towards evening they went out for a walk and finally, they sat down to a supper prepared for them by Beauty. And they even scolded her when she didn't cook to their taste.

And so it went until one day, the good merchant received news that one of his ships, which he had thought was lost, had returned safely from over the sea with a rich cargo. The merchant was delighted and at once he made ready to go to the city. Before his departure, he asked each of his daughters what they would like him to bring them when he returned.

"A chest of new gowns," demanded the oldest.

"A box of beautiful jewels," said the second.

But Beauty was silent and said nothing. She knew very well that her father would have other things to attend to than buying clothes and jewellery. The merchant knew what she was thinking, but he asked her anyway.

"And what about you, Beauty. Don't you want anything?"

"No, Father, I have everything I need," she replied, "unless you could bring me a rose, for none grow here."

Her sisters burst out laughing. "You should have asked for a new wooden spoon! Or a new broom!" they cried.

But the merchant ignored their ridicule. He kissed his daughter on the brow and said, "I shall bring you a rose, Beauty. And I shall be back in a week."

And just as he had promised, within a week, the merchant was ready to return. His ship had arrived safely in harbour, but when he had sold all his goods and paid all his debts, there was scarcely enough left for the new gowns and jewellery for his elder daughters. And so he was just as poor as before. Very sadly he set out for home.

On his way through a deep woods, he was caught by a storm. The heavens turned black, lightning flashed among the clouds, the wind bent the trees almost to the ground, and wolves howled on every side. The poor merchant became hopelessly lost and was certain that his end had come.

Just when the storm was at its worst, he saw a light shining through the trees. He urged his horse in that direction and soon he found himself before the gates of a huge castle. The merchant was amazed, for he had never heard that a beautiful castle stood in this forest. Boldly, he rode into the courtyard, jumped down from his horse, and strode up to the door, intending to knock and ask for shelter for the night. But as he raised his hand to knock, the door swung open by itself, as though inviting him to come in.

The merchant entered as if in a dream, for one door after another opened up, and he walked through corridor after corridor until at last, he found himself in a large, magnificent hall. A fire was burning cheerfully on the hearth and beside it there was a table laid with everything a hungry man could ask for. He waited a while to see whether anyone would come, but he heard not a voice nor a footfall. And so the good merchant took courage, sat down at the table, ate and drank his fill, and then set out to explore the castle once more.

And again, one door after another opened up before him, and he walked through corridor after corridor until at last he found himself in a beautiful bed-chamber. In one corner of the room, a huge fire was burning on the hearth, and in another, there was a soft four-poster bed. The merchant plucked up his courage, lay down in the bed and fell into a peaceful sleep.

When he awoke in the morning, breakfast awaited him on a little table beside his bed, and when he had eaten, he found a clean suit of clothes on a chair. The merchant dressed and then went to look for his horse. He found it in the stable, stamping contentedly in a stall before a manger full of hay. The merchant led it into the courtyard, jumped into the saddle, turned once more to the castle, and with a wave of his broad-brimmed hat, cried out, "Thank you for the hospitality, my unknown host! A thousand times thank you, and farewell!"

And he urged his horse to a trot. As he was riding under an arbour by the gate, however, a rose-bud caught in his saddle, and the merchant suddenly remembered Beauty's wish. He had gifts for both the older sisters, but he had completely forgotten about the rose for Beauty. Without thinking any more about it, he leaned out of the saddle and picked the rose bud. But it was a grave mistake, for no sooner had he touched the bud than a terrific clamour arose, as though the whole world were collapsing around him. When the noise died down and the merchant had recovered his senses, a frightful Beast was standing before him.

"Ungrateful wretch!" roared the Beast. "I welcomed you to my castle, I fed you and gave you a bed for the night, and now you thank me by taking what I like most in this world. You shall pay for this with your life!"

The merchant was terrified, and he fell on his knees and pleaded, "Do not be angry, kind sir! I could not know that you would be so enraged over a single rose bud. I promised my daughter that I would bring her a rose as a present, and so I picked one of yours. Have mercy on me, kind sir!"

But the Beast was unmoved. "Do not call me kind sir!" he roared. "I am the Beast. Sweet words will not soften my heart. Now your life is in my hands and nothing can save you, unless you give me one of your daughters instead. You must bring her to me within three days or return yourself! Swear to it!"

The merchant had no intention of bringing the Beast one of his daughters, but he saw his chance to escape, and so he agreed. "I swear that within three days I shall bring you one of my daughters, or return myself," he said.

The Beast was satisfied. "I shall expect you," he said. "And so that you will not return home empty-handed, go once more into the castle. There, in the first room, you will find a coffer full of gold, silver and precious stones. It is my gift to your daughters."

And before the merchant could recover his senses and thank the Beast, he was gone. The merchant went back into the castle and in the first room he found a coffer full of jewellery on a table. It was so heavy that he could hardly lift it, and it was all the poor horse could do to carry it.

The merchant returned home with a heavy heart, but his two elder daughters noticed nothing, for they could think only of the gifts he was bringing.

"Have you the new gowns for us, Father?" asked the eldest.

"And the jewels?" demanded the second.

"I have, I have," sighed the merchant. "And I even have a rose for Beauty. That was the most costly gift of all."

And he told his daughters what had happened to him in the charmed castle in the middle of the woods.

"The Beast wants one of you, but rather than give him any of you, I would go back there myself."

At this both the elder sisters began to protest. "Why should you go back to the Beast, Father?" they cried. "Let Beauty go. She's the cause of it all. She wanted a rose, so let her have it, thorns and all. What would become of us without you? Who would buy us new clothes and jewellery?"

Then Beauty spoke up. "My sisters are right, Father. It was my fault and I shall pay the price for it. Take me to this Beast. Who knows, perhaps he will have mercy on me."

At first the merchant would not even hear of such a thing, but finally he relented, and the third day he set out with Beauty for the charmed castle in the middle of the woods. The older sisters wiped their eyes when the farewells were said, but their tears were none too sincere.

"Good luck," the oldest sister called after Beauty.

"Give our greetings to your Beast," cried the second. And then they both ran to get dressed for their afternoon walk.

And while her elder sisters were gaily getting ready for their walk, poor Beauty rode sadly with her Father towards the castle in the middle of the woods. The thickets opened up before them as though an unseen hand were pushing them aside, and the horses ran as though someone were leading them by the halter.

Almost before they knew it, they were standing in the courtyard of the beautiful castle. When they jumped down from their horses and entered, the doors opened one after the other and they walked down one corridor after another until they found themselves in the beautiful hall. A fire was burning cheerily on the hearth, and before the fire stood a table laid with everything the guests could ask for. It was nearly evening, and so the merchant and Beauty ate and then sat down in front of the fire.

At the stroke of seven, a terrific clamour suddenly arose, as though the whole world were collapsing around them, and before Beauty and the merchant could recover their senses, the terrible Beast was standing before them.

"Welcome," roared the Beast. "I am glad, merchant, that you kept your word, and I am glad, Beauty, that you have come to me. Tomorrow you must part with your Father and then we shall be alone together for ever. In the meantime, goodnight!"

And before Beauty could say anything, before she could wish him a goodnight, the Beast was gone. The merchant and Beauty once more set out through the castle, and once more the doors opened for them and they walked along one corridor after another until they came to a door with the words "The Room of My Beloved Beauty" written on it.

Beauty entered the room as if in a dream. When she lived in the city with her father, they had had a beautiful house, but she had never seen such a beautiful bed-chamber in her life before. In one corner a fire was burning merrily on the hearth, and in the other corner there was a soft four-poster bed. Beauty lay down in it and slept peacefully until morning.

In the morning, the merchant said farewell to his daughter. With tears in their eyes, they embraced, then he jumped on his horse and rode through the gate, and before Beauty could wipe her eyes dry, the woods had closed over him like water over a stone, and he was gone.

And so Beauty was left alone in the castle. There was plenty for her to do, and the time passed quickly. She walked from room to room and from hall to hall, and before she had explored half the castle, it was midday, and a fully-laid table was already awaiting her in the dining room. Unseen servants brought her anything she desired, unseen hands put the best morsels on her plate, filled her cup, and carried the empty dishes away.

At noon, Beauty found the table laid for dinner, and in the evening, the table was laden with a magnificent supper. Just as she was sitting down to eat, she heard the sound of heavy footsteps behind her, making the castle tremble and shake until she was certain it would collapse. It was the Beast.

"Beauty," he said, "may I sit down to supper with you?"

Beauty was frightened, but she replied pluckily, "Why do you ask, Beast? You are the master here."

"No, I am not," said the Beast. "Only you give the orders here. If I disturb you, you have only to say so and I shall leave. Tell me, are you afraid of me?"

Beauty could not lie. "I am, Beast. You are very frightful to look at, but I think you have a good heart."

And at this, the Beast asked, "Tell me the truth, Beauty, will you marry me?"

"Oh no, Beast," cried Beauty in alarm. "Do not ask that of me."

The Beast let out a terrible roar, as though someone had plunged a knife into his heart, but then he hung his head sadly and said, "In that case, Beauty, good night!"

And before Beauty could reply, before she could wish him a goodnight too, the Beast was gone. Beauty was unhappy to have caused him so much grief, but what could she do? Sadly, she lay down to sleep in her soft white four-poster bed, sadly she tossed and turned, but when at last she fell asleep, she slept peacefully until morning.

And so the days went by. Every morning, she found new clothes beside her bed, every midday she had a fine meal, and every evening she talked a while with the Beast. He came each evening on the stroke of seven and it wasn't long before Beauty found that she could hardly wait for him to come. Even though he was terribly frightening to look at, she enjoyed sitting and talking with him and listening to what he told her. Only one thing made her very sad, for every evening, just before the Beast bade her good night, he would ask, "Answer me truthfully, Beauty. Will you marry me?"

And though she regretted it, she had to tell him each time that she wouldn't, that she could never ever marry him.

One day, she said, "Please, Beast, don't expect me to marry you, and please don't ask me to every evening. You only make me suffer, and you suffer too."

And the Beast replied, "Then promise me at least that you will never leave me."

Beauty lowered her head sadly and replied, "I would like to promise you that, Beast, but I am afraid that I will die here of homesickness. I long to see my Father again, and I know he is longing to see me. Let me go home for a few days."

The Beast could not refuse. "I shall let you go, Beauty," he said, "but you must come back within three days. If you were not to return, I would die of grief. Here is a ring. When you want to come back, put it on the table beside your bed and in the morning you will be here again. Until then, good night."

And before Beauty could utter a word, before she could wish him a good night as well, the Beast was gone. Only his ring remained on the table. Beauty slipped it on her finger and went to bed.

In the morning, when she woke up, she didn't know whether she was awake or still dreaming. She was lying in her dear old bed in her father's house. Everything was as it was before, the bed, the table, the wardrobe, the chair. Only she was different. She had on a beautiful dress, the kind she wore in the Beast's castle, and she had silver slippers on her feet and golden rings on her fingers, such as she had never worn at home.

Just then the door opened and in came her beloved father and her two elder sisters. Her father embraced her warmly, while her sisters merely stared at her in envy.

"What a beautiful dress you have, Beauty," said the eldest.

"And what magnificent jewellery you have," said the younger sister.

"The Beast has looked after you well," they cried out in unison, and because they were envious of Beauty's good fortune, they immediately began to think of ways to spoil it. As soon as they learned that she had to return to the castle in three days, they tried to persuade her to stay at home.

"Why should you return so soon, Beauty?" they said. "Stay here with us a week at least. The Beast won't eat you up."

And they pleaded and begged and coaxed and cajoled for so long that Beauty finally gave in.

And so when the three days were up, she did not return to the castle. And when the fourth day had come and gone, Beauty was still at home. And after a fifth day had gone by, Beauty had a nightmare. She dreamed that her Beast lay grieving in a corner of the castle garden. Beauty awoke with tears in her eyes, resolving to return to him without delay.

"I only hope it is not too late," she said to herself, and the whole day long she walked about like a body without a soul, for she could hardly wait for evening to come. And as soon as it was dark, she went to bed, putting the Beast's ring on her table.

In the morning when she woke up, she didn't know whether she was really awake or still dreaming. She was lying in her bed in the castle and everything was as it was before. The fire was burning merrily on the hearth, a new dress was lying on the chair, and breakfast awaited her on the table. But the castle was somehow different. It seemed emptier and more forlorn. Weeping, Beauty jumped out of bed and ran to look for the Beast.

She searched for a long time, running through all the corridors, looking through all the rooms, walking around the whole garden, but nowhere could she find him. At last, when she came to the very end of the garden, she saw the Beast lying lifeless in the grass.

Beauty was terrified, for her dream had been true. She threw herself upon the Beast weeping and embraced him and said, "Forgive me, Beast, for hurting you. I didn't really want to. Wake up, I beg of you, and I shall do anything you ask. I shall marry you with pleasure, if that is what you wish."

And suddenly a great clamour arose, as though the whole world were collapsing, and when Beauty came to her senses, there before her stood a dashing young Prince.

"Thank you, Beauty, for your goodness has saved me. Your love has broken the evil charm. An old witch changed me into a terrible Beast, and you have freed me. If you wish, tomorrow you may be my wife and the Queen of my kingdom."

And at that moment a crowd of lords and ladies and faithful servants came running from the castle, and they all thanked Beauty for freeing them from the power of the evil witch. The empty castle came alive, the desolate woods changed into a flowering city, and everywhere peals of laughter and song sounded, just like at a gay wedding.

But the wedding came three days later, after the Prince's servants, pages, cooks, and chamberlains had made the proper preparations. And when it was finally held, all the effort was worth it, for truly, Beauty and her Prince had the most magnificent wedding the world had ever seen.

When it was over, they all lived happily ever after. Except for Beauty's two older sisters. They were never ever happy and content, and ever afterwards they wished that they had gone to live with the Beast themselves, and that instead of gowns and fine jewels, they had asked for a rose bud.

a merrily bubbling well and from that well a man was drinking. But it was not a man like other men, for this man seemed made of flowers.

The Red King spurred his horse towards him, but he could not catch the Man of Flowers, for as soon as he heard the thundering of hooves behind him, the Man of Flowers raised his head and vanished as if he had dissolved into thin air.

From that time on, the Red King could think of nothing else but the Man of Flowers. His company of hunters soon noticed this, and one day the oldest of the royal hunters came before the King and said, "Great King, we know what is troubling you, but if it is your wish, we shall end your sorrow and bring you this Man of Flowers."

The King was overjoyed. "Bring him to me and you shall be amply rewarded," he said. "But tell me, how do you expect to catch him?"

"Leave that up to us, Great King," replied the royal hunter. "Simply order your servants to give us the best barrel of wine from the royal cellars."

And so the King issued an order for the hunters to be given whatever they asked for, and then they set out with the barrel of wine for the well under the oak tree. They drew all the water out of the well and poured the wine in its place. Then they hid themselves in the bushes to wait.

They did not have to wait long, for soon the Man of Flowers appeared, looked around, and then leaned down to the well to drink.

The wine in the well was delicious. The Man of Flowers had never tasted anything so good before. "Ah, the water today is excellent," he cried delightedly, and he drank and he drank until his head was spinning.

"Now for a little nap," he said, and he stretched out on the moss and immediately fell asleep, as soundly as a log.

And now the hunters had no trouble catching the Man of Flowers. They sprang out of the bushes, bound him tightly, and then carried him off in great pomp to the royal palace.

No words can describe the Red King's happiness. He put the Man of Flowers into a tower in the courtyard of the palace, locked the door with nine locks, and carried the keys around on his belt all day long. He entrusted them to no one, and he himself took the Man of Flowers food and drink. Each day, the King would sit with him, asking him who and what he was. But the Man of Flowers would not reply. He scarcely ate, he scarcely drank, and he never ever spoke. It was as if he were deaf and dumb. He would just sit at the barred window looking sadly out towards the woods beyond the palace.

The Red King knew very well what the Man of Flowers was longing for, but he showed him no mercy. He was proud to have something that no one else in the world had, and he continually invited guests from near and far so that he could show off his rare and prized possession.

As I say, the King did not feel the least bit sorry for the Man of Flowers, but his little son Prince Johnny had a softer heart. Whenever he had the chance, he would run to the tower, seat himself on a rock and watch the Man of Flowers looking sadly out of the window towards the woods beyond the castle. And when no one was watching him, when no one was listening, he would try to cheer the Man of Flowers up.

"Man of Flowers," he would say, "don't be so sad! Man of Flowers, speak with me and you'll feel better!"

But the Man of Flowers would not even look at Johnny, nor did he respond to his plea. He just kept on staring at the woods beyond the castle.

One day, however, he unexpectedly spoke. That very day the Red King had left to ride to the borders of his kingdom to welcome a noble guest. The little Prince was alone in the palace and at once he hurried to the tower. The Man of Flowers was sitting at the window as usual, and as usual, Prince Johnny tried to cheer him up.

"Man of Flowers, don't be so sad. Man of Flowers, speak with me at least, and you will feel better."

And then the Man of Flowers turned to the little Prince and said in a quiet voice, "I shall never feel better as long as I am here. I can only be happy at home in my own woods. Let me go, Prince!"

The little Prince was dismayed. "How can I let you go when I don't have the keys? My father the King carries them around on his belt all day."

But the Man of Flowers replied, "At night he puts them under his pillow, and this morning he forgot to take them with him. Run and fetch them, Prince. Let me out, and I shall reward you. When you grow up, I shall give you a princess for your wife such as no king in the world has ever had."

The little Prince did not ignore the Man of Flower's plea. He ran quickly to the Red King's bed-chamber, reached under the pillow and sure enough, there were the keys to the tower. The little Prince took them, returned to the tower, and opened the nine locks.

The Man of Flowers ran out of the tower crying, "Thank you, Prince Johnny! I will keep my promise to you, you may count on it, and if you ever need help, remember me and I will come. Farewell!"

And before the Prince could reply, before he could utter a word, the Man of Flowers had gone, vanished as though he had dissolved into thin air. Prince Johnny was left alone with the keys to the tower in his hand. He ran to his father's bed-chamber to put them back, but that did not help very much. The Man of Flowers was gone, and the Red King was already riding into the palace with his noble guest.

No words can describe the King's terrible rage when he found the tower empty. He called all his servants and rebuked them all so soundly that the truth soon came out.

"Be not angry, Great King," his servants said, "but it was your son Prince Johnny who let the Man of Flowers go."

The King was overcome with wrath and shouted, "Such a great wrong-doing deserves a great punishment."

And then he commanded his old and faithful servant to take the Prince into the woods and kill him there. "But woe unto you if you do not obey! As proof that you have killed him, bring me back his heart."

The next day the faithful servant awoke the little Prince as soon as it was light. "Get up, Prince," he said. "Today we are going into the woods."

The little Prince suspected nothing. Gaily he got up, gaily he dressed, gaily he whistled to his dog and then he set off with the faithful old servant into the woods. They walked on for a long time, they walked the whole day and as they went, the old servant became sadder and sadder. The burden of his terrible duty lay heavy upon him, for though he did not want to kill the little Prince, he feared disobeying the King even more.

And then Prince Johnny finally asked him, "What is the matter, faithful servant? Why are you so sad? And where is this long journey taking us?"

With tears in his eyes, the old servant replied, "I have brought you into the woods to kill you, Prince. The King your father, commanded it, and as proof I am to bring him your heart."

The little Prince was frightened and began to cry. "Do not kill me, faithful servant! Let me go, and I shall go wherever my legs shall take me. And instead of my heart, you can take my father the heart of my dog."

The faithful servant took mercy on the Prince. He killed the poor dog, cut out his heart, and then said farewell to the young lad. The servant returned to the Red King's castle, and the prince set off through the deep woods, going wherever his legs would take him.

How long he walked, how long he wandered through the woods, pushing his way through bushes and thickets, eating roots and drinking water from woodland springs, no one knows. And when at last, tattered and torn and hungry, he came out of the forest, he saw before him a wondrous thing. In the middle of a flowering meadow stood a magnificent palace with golden roofs, silver walls, and windows of pure crystal, and it all glittered with a brilliant, blinding light. Only one thing marred this beauty. In front of the palace stood a hundred columns and on each of ninety-nine of them there was a human head.

Prince Johnny was alarmed, and he would much rather have taken to his heels and run away. But where? On all sides there was a dense forest where he would die of hunger. And so he gathered his courage together and pounded on the palace gate, thump, thump, thump, and shouted out, "Open up, good people, and give work to a poor wanderer!"

The gates of the palace swung open and on the threshold stood the lord of the house himself, the Yellow King.

"Come in, young man," he said.

"If it is work you seek, you may have it. Here a year lasts only three days, and if you serve me well, you shall have everything you need for the rest of your life. But if not, then I shall have your head impaled on a stake in front of the castle. Well?"

What could the poor Prince do? It was either die like an animal in the woods or enter the service of the Yellow King.

And so he bravely went into the palace. The King led him to a hall, seated him at a table, and ordered supper to be brought.

"You must certainly be hungry and thirsty after such a long journey," he said.

"That I am," replied Prince Johnny truthfully, but he ate very little, for no sooner had he cut himself a slice of bread than the King's daughter came into the room. She was even younger than Prince Johnny, but though she was young, she was as beautiful as a spring day; though her forehead was covered with a veil and her smock was buttoned up to her neck, so that only her eyes and mouth could be seen, she still shone like the sun itself.

She brought Johnny a jug of wine, but the Prince hardly touched it. He had eyes only for the beautiful little Princess. But the Princess was impatient. "Eat quickly, young man," she said, "or I shall blow out the lamp."

"Just a little longer," pleaded Johnny, "until I eat this crust and drink this glass."

But the Princess lost patience. She blew out the lamp and went out of the room, and the poor prince was left alone in the dark and had to go to bed hungry.

Next morning his work began. And it was not easy, you may believe it. The King gave him a cart and told him that he had to bring it back the same evening full of grass from the rock mountain which lay to the north of the palace. The King's golden horse would eat no other grass. But on that mountain there nested a huge eagle, and whoever strayed onto the mountain or dared to go there was torn to pieces by the eagle and fed to his young.

"Now you know all you need to know," said the Yellow King, and he went with Johnny to the door. "But remember, if you come back empty-handed, I'll have your head impaled on a stake."

And so the poor Prince set out for the rock mountain. He trudged along very slowly, and why should he have hurried, for on the mountain a huge eagle was awaiting him, and in the palace there was the Yellow King! And then, just when he was feeling most down-hearted, he remembered the Man of Flowers.

"O Man of Flowers," he sighed, "if you were only here, perhaps you could help me. And anyway, I'm in this mess all because of you."

Almost before his sigh had died away, Prince Johnny saw a wondrous thing ahead of him. A thicket by the side of the path opened and out stepped the Man of Flowers.

"What is the matter, Prince? Why are you sighing?" he asked.

"Why should I not sigh, Man of Flowers," answered the Prince. "The Yellow King has sent me to fetch grass from yonder mountain, but if I go there, the eagle will certainly tear me to pieces, and if I don't bring the grass back, the King will have my head impaled on a stake."

The Man of Flowers only laughed.

"There's nothing to fear, Prince," he said. "I shall help you. Follow this little path here until you come to my house. There you shall find my mother, and you may chat with her and leave the rest to me."

Prince Johnny ran along the pathway until he came to a beautiful flower-garden, and in the middle of the flower-garden stood an even more beautiful castle made entirely of flowers. And at the castle gate was standing an old, white-haired woman.

"Welcome, Prince Johnny," she said in a kindly voice. "I thought you were never coming."

The white-haired old woman led the Prince inside, fed him well, had a nice chat with him, and finally she gave him a golden spindle which spun all by itself.

"It will come in handy, Prince, you'll see," she said. "But run along now. My son is waiting for you."

158

And sure enough, the Man of Flowers was waiting at the foot of the rock mountain. "Here is the grass, Prince," he said. "Now you can go home without any fear."

Prince Johnny thanked him from the bottom of his heart, took the cart by the handle and gaily set off for the palace of the Yellow King.

The King was waiting for him, and when he saw the Prince returning with a cart full of grass, he was very pleased. "I see that you are a real man, Johnny," he said. "Now you have one day's service behind you. Come in and have supper, for you must be hungry after such hard work."

"That I am," replied Prince Johnny truthfully, but he ate very little, for no sooner had he sat down at the table and cut himself a slice of bread than the King's daughter came into the room. Even though she had a veil on her forehead and her smock buttoned up to her neck, she shone like the sun itself.

She brought Johnny a jug of wine, but the poor Prince hardly tasted it: he had eyes only for the beautiful little Princess. But the Princess was becoming impatient.

"Eat more quickly, young man, or I shall blow the lamp out," she said sternly.

"Blow it out if you wish, Princess," he replied. "I shall eat in the dark. We servants are used to such things."

The Princess lost all patience, blew the lamp out, and retired to her chambers. But Prince Johnny did not remain in the dark for long. He took the golden spindle which he had received as a gift out of his basket and placed it on the table. The spindle shone brighter than the brightest lamp and what is more, it spun a golden thread. Prince Johnny could eat and drink as much as he wished without interruption.

The golden spindle shone so brightly that even the Princess in her chambers noticed the light. She sent a chambermaid to see what the new servant was using to light his room. In a little while, the chambermaid ran back, quite out of breath.

"Princess, I looked through the window and I saw the most wondrous thing. That new servant of ours has a golden spindle on his table."

At first, the Princess did not want to believe this. With her veil over her forehead and her smock buttoned up to her neck, she ran to Johnny's room to see for herself. And sure enough, the King's new servant had a golden spindle on the table in front of him and that spindle was shining brighter than the brightest lamp and what was more, it was spinning a golden thread.

"I must have that spindle," said the Princess. "What do you want for it, young man?"

And Prince Johnny replied, "All I ask for it is that you take off your veil and show me your forehead."

At first the Princess refused. She offered Johnny everything she could think of, gold, silver, precious stones, but the Prince insisted. Finally the Princess gave in. She flung aside the veil over her forehead and the room filled up with light as when a burning lamp is brought into a dark place. For under the veil, the Princess had a golden star on her forehead.

"There, you have seen what you wanted to see," she said indignantly, and she snatched up the golden spindle and was gone. Prince Johnny was left alone in the dark and had to go to bed. But he did not regret what he had done.

159

The next day his duties began again. Once more, the King sent him with the cart for grass from the rock mountain.

"But remember," he warned, "if you return empty-handed, I shall have your head impaled on a stake."

So the poor Prince set out on the familiar path to the rock mountain. He trudged along very slowly, and why should he have hurried, when the huge eagle was waiting for him on the mountain and in the palace there was the Yellow King! Just when he was feeling his worst, he remembered the Man of Flowers.

"O Man of Flowers," he sighed. "If you were only here, perhaps you could help me. And anyway, I'm in this mess all because of you."

Even before his sigh had died away, the Man of Flowers was standing before Johnny. "What's the matter now, Prince," he asked.

"Why are you sighing? You know I'll help you, so don't be afraid. Just go to my mother's and leave the rest to me."

And so Johnny once more ran along the little pathway to the beautiful castle in the middle of the flower-garden. The white-haired old lady was already waiting for him by the gate. She took him inside, gave him a good meal and had a nice talk with him, and finally she gave the Prince three golden apples as a gift.

"They will come in handy, Prince, you'll see," she said. "But run along now. My son is waiting for you."

And sure enough, the Man of Flowers was waiting below the rock moutain. "Here is the grass, Prince," he said. "Now you can go home without fear."

Prince Johnny thanked him, took the cart by the handle, and went merrily back to the palace of the Yellow King.

The King was waiting for him, and when he saw the Prince returning with a cart full of grass, he was pleased. "I see that you are a real man, Johnny. Now you have two days of service behind you. Come in and have supper. You must be hungry after such a hard day's work."

"That I am," replied Prince Johnny truthfully, but again he ate only very little, for no sooner had he sat down at the table and cut himself a slice of bread than the King's daughter came into the room. Even though her smock was buttoned up to her neck and her forehead was covered with a veil as usual, she shone like the sun itself.

She brought Johnny a jug of wine, but the poor Prince hardly tasted it: he only had eyes for the beautiful little Princess. As for the Princess, she was running out of patience.

"Eat quickly, young man," she said, "or I shall blow out the lamp."

"Blow it out if you wish, Princess," replied Johnny. "I shall eat in the dark. We servants are used to such things."

The Princess lost all her patience, blew out the lamp and retired to her chambers. But Prince Johnny did not remain in the dark for long. He took the golden apples which he had received as a present, and put them on the table. The apples shone brighter than the brightest lamp, and what was more, they smelled sweeter than a whole apple-orchard. Prince Johnny could eat as much as he wished without interruption.

The golden apples on the table shone so brightly that even the Princess herself

160

noticed the light. She sent a chambermaid to see what the new servant was using to light his room. In a little while, the chambermaid ran back quite out of breath.

"Princess, that new servant had three golden apples on his table," she cried.

At first the Princess did not want to believe it. With her veil on her forehead and her smock buttoned up to her neck, she ran into Johnny's room to see for herself. And sure enough, the King's new servant had three golden apples on the table in front of him and the apples smelled sweeter than any apple-orchard.

"I must have those apples," said the Princess. "What do you want for them, young man?"

"Nothing more than for you to unbutton that smock of yours and show me your left shoulder," replied Johnny.

At first the Princess refused. She offered Johnny everything she could think of: gold, silver, precious stones, but the Prince insisted. Finally the Princess gave in. She unbuttoned her smock and the whole room filled with a glowing light, as when two burning lamps are taken into a dark place. For underneath her smock, on her left shoulder, the Princess had a golden moon.

"There, you have seen what you wanted to see," she said indignantly, and she snatched up the golden apples and was gone. Prince Johnny was left alone in the dark and had to go to bed. Bet he did not regret what he had done.

The third day his duties began again. For the third time, the King sent him with the cart to the rock mountain for grass.

"But remember," he warned, "if you return empty-handed, I shall have your head impaled on a stake."

So the poor Prince set out once more on the familiar path to the rock mountain. He trudged along very slowly, but why should he have hurried, when the eagle was waiting for him on the mountain, and in the palace there was the Yellow King. Just when he was feeling his worse, he remembered the Man of Flowers again.

"Oh, if only you were here," he sighed, "perhaps you could help me."

And before his sigh had died out, the Man of Flowers was standing before him. "What's the matter now, Prince?" he asked. "Why are you sighing. You know I'll help you, so don't be afraid. Just go to my mother's and leave the rest to me."

And so for the third time the Prince ran down the pathway to the beautiful castle in the middle of the garden full of flowers. The old white-haired lady was waiting for him at the gate. She took him inside, gave him a good meal and had a nice chat with him, and finally she gave him a gift of a golden mother hen with little golden chicks.

"They will come in handy, Prince, you'll see," she said. "But run along now, my son is waiting for you. And if we don't see each other again, farewell and think well of us!"

"That I will, and with gratitude," Johnny promised, and he hurried off to the rock mountain where the Man of Flowers was waiting for him.

"Here is the grass, Prince," he said. "Now you can go home without fear. And when you marry, don't forget to invite me to the wedding!"

Prince Johnny thanked him, said farewell to the Man of Flowers, and hurried back to the palace of the Yellow King with the cart.

The King was waiting for him, and when he saw the Prince returning with a cart full of grass, he was very pleased. "I see that you are a real man, Johnny," he said. "Now your work is done and tomorrow, I shall pay you. But now come in and have supper, you must be hungry after such hard work."

"That I am," replied Johnny truthfully, but even then he did not eat much. For as soon as he sat down to the table and cut himself a slice of bread, the King's daughter came into the room, and though she had the veil over her forehead as usual and her smock buttoned up to her neck, she shone like the sun.

She brought Johnny a jug of wine, but once more the poor Prince hardly tasted it for he still had eyes only for the beautiful little Princess. But she was as impatient as ever.

"Eat more quickly, young man," she said, "or I shall blow out this lamp."

"Blow it out if you wish, Princess," replied Johnny. "I shall eat in the dark. We servants are used to such things."

The Princess lost patience completely, blew out the lamp and went to her chambers. But the Prince did not remain in the dark for long. He took the golden mother hen and her little golden chicks out of the basket and set them on the table. They shone more brightly than the brightest lamp and what was more they clucked and peeped so music-ally that it was a joy to hear. Prince Johnny could eat and drink in peace to his heart's content.

The golden mother hen shone so brightly that the Princess in her chambers noticed it. She sent a chambermaid to discover what the new servant was using to light his room this time. In a little while, the chambermaid came running back all out of breath.

"Princess," she cried, "the new servant has a golden hen and little golden chickens."

At first, the Princess didn't want to believe it. With her veil over her forehead and her smock buttoned up to her neck, she ran to his room to see for herself. And sure enough, the King's new servant had a golden hen with little golden chicks on the table before him, and they clucked and peeped so musically that it was a joy to hear.

"I must have that hen and her chicks," said the Princess. "What do you want for them?"

"Nothing more than for you to unbutton that smock of yours and show me your right shoulder," replied Prince Johnny.

At first the Princess refused. She offered Johnny everything she could think of: gold, silver, precious stones, but the prince insisted. Finally the princess gave in. She unbut-toned her smock and the whole room filled with a glowing light as when three bright lamps are taken into a dark place. For under her smock, on her right shoulder, the Princess had a golden sun.

"There, you have seen what you wanted to see," said the Princess angrily, and she snatched up the golden hen and the chicks and was gone. Prince Johnny was left alone in the dark and had to go to bed. But he didn't regret what he had done.

The next morning, the Yellow King called Johnny to him, gave him a good horse, a sharp sword, a new cloak and a pouch of ducats and said, "This is for serving me well, Johnny. Use them well, and take a look round the world. But when you return, don't forget to pay us a visit!"

And then the Yellow King bade Johnny a warm farewell. But the little Princess did not come to say goodbye. She only looked at him through her window, and when Johnny rode through the castle gates on his beautiful horse, with his cloak over his shoulder and his sword by his side, she said, "If I didn't know he was just a servant, I would swear he was a handsome prince."

And so Prince Johnny went into the world. He rode about the world for seven long years, from river to river, from mountain to mountain, from town to town, from one kingdom to the next. And in those seven years, the little Prince grew into a strong young man, as sturdy as an oak. Even his own father would not have recognized him. The good Prince decided the time had come to return home, and so he turned his horse around, urged it to a gallop, and started homewards.

How long he rode, how long he wandered over mountains, across rivers and through woods, no words can describe. And when at last, weary and exhausted, he came out of the mountains and forests, he saw before him a wondrous thing. In the middle of a flowering meadow stood a magnificent palace with golden roofs, silver walls and windows of crystal, and it glittered with a brilliant, blinding light. And what made it even more beautiful were the many splendid coaches and riders on horse-back waiting outside.

And it was no wonder. For this was the palace of the Yellow King and these guests in the coaches and on horse-back were all young men who had come to seek the hand of the King's beautiful daughter. In those seven years she had grown into such a lovely princess that it took one's breath away just to look at her. Even though she still went around with a veil over her forehead and with her smock buttoned up to her neck, she was more beautiful than a spring day. And because it was time for her to marry, the King had proclaimed that he would give his daughter to the one who could guess what birthmarks the Princess had.

Ever since the announcement, the Yellow King's palace was like a carnival. From all corners of the world, they came to try their luck: kings and knights, rich gentlemen and farm-boys. But as many as came in glory and high expectation, as many went away in shame, for no one could guess what birthmarks the Princess had.

Prince Johnny saw that his time had come. He appeared before the King just as he was, in his ragged cloak and worn-out boots. He bowed deeply and said, "Great King, I know what birthmarks your daughter has."

The Yellow King looked at him closely, for it seemed to him that he had seen this man's face before, and that he had heard that voice somewhere before. "Well, speak up, young man! If you really know, then the Princess will be yours."

At this Prince Johnny replied, "Your daughter, Great King, has three birthmarks. On her forehead, she has a golden star, on her left shoulder she has a golden moon, and on her right shoulder a golden sun. That is why she shines so brightly, even though she goes about all the time with a veil on her forehead and her smock buttoned up to her neck."

The Yellow King had to admit that this stranger was speaking the truth. "You have guessed correctly, young man," he said, "and my daughter is yours. But tell me, who are you?"

And Prince Johnny replied, "Seven years ago a boy served you, Great King, and that boy brought you three carts full of grass from the rock mountain and he gave your daughter three gifts. When he went away, you invited him to visit you on his way back. And now he is standing before you."

And at last the Yellow King recognized him. "So it is you, Johnny!"

"Yes, Great King," replied Prince Johnny, "it's me."

And so, just as the Man of Flowers had promised, Prince Johnny received the most beautiful princess in all the world as his wife. The Yellow King held a great wedding, and he invited kings from all over the world to come. Among them came the Red King, ruler of the neighbouring Red Kingdom. He was by now old and bent, and it was a wonder that Johnny recognized him. The Red King, however, did not recognize Johnny at all, and so they sat together at one table, like strangers.

When the wedding was at its best and when the wine had loosened the guests' tongues, the groom stood up and asked each of the guests to tell something about his own life, whether merry or sad. The guests did not wait to be asked twice. Each in turn

told something from his experiences, and often the tales were wonderful indeed. And finally it came the Red King's turn.

The Red King thought for a while, and then said, "My story is not a happy one, but if I must tell you something, then I will tell you what burdens my heart."

And then he began to tell of his little son and the Man of Flowers, how he had locked him in a tower, and how the little Prince had let him go. And then, with tears in his eyes, the old King went on, "And as a punishment, I had my own little son taken into the woods and killed. My servant brought his heart back to me as proof."

Everyone at the table fell silent, for the Red King's tale was a sad one indeed. But the groom merely smiled and said, "And supposing it were not your son's heart, but the heart of his dog? Supposing your son was alive and standing here before you right now?"

For the first time the Red King lifted his eyes and looked closely into the groom's face. And then he recognized him. "Is that really you, Johnny?" he asked in amazement.

Prince Johnny stepped up to his father, embraced him and said, "Yes, Father, it's me." And from that moment on, the wedding was twice as merry as before. The Yellow King was delighted to have such a powerful son-in-law, the Princess was overjoyed to have a prince as her husband, Johnny was very glad to see his father again, but the Red King was happiest of all, because he had found his son once more.

And what about the Man of Flowers, you say? He came to the wedding too, for Prince Johnny did not forget his promise. And how could he have, when he had so much to be grateful to him for, especially for his beautiful bride? But after the wedding, no one ever saw him again, not even Prince Johnny, and so from that time on they tell about him only in fairy-tales.

WILLIE COUNTED THE DAYS ON HIS FINGERS.
Friday, Saturday, Sunday. All morning he went through his books, so that he would have the best tales for the end. He tried to remember everything his Granny used to read him or tell him, and after he had picked out the ones he wanted, and marked them with book-marks, he went outside to play.

He was outside all afternoon and in the evening he was as hungry as a wolf. Granny was delighted. "I see," she said, "that you're perfectly all right again."

And then she sent him to bed. When she was tucking him in, Willie asked if he could read for a little while.

Granny laughed. "You've never asked me before," she said.

But she turned on his bed-side lamp and then went out.

When she was gone, Willie turned the lamp out again. As soon as he sat down on the bear-skin rug with the book on his lap, a few sparks flew out of the fire and there was the little girl sitting on the mantle-piece.

"Well," she said, "did you enjoy yourself outside this afternoon?"

Willie was surprised. "You saw me outside? Where were you?"

But the little girl only laughed and replied, "Curiosity killed the cat!"

But she didn't feel much like playing hide-and-seek or tag. "Read to me instead," she said.

This was what Willie was waiting for. He opened the book at the book-mark and began to read very slowly and clearly. And this is what he read.

THE LITTLE SOLDIER AND THE LAMP WITH THE BLUE LIGHT

Once upon a time there was a little soldier. He was as sturdy as a pine tree, gay, courageous, and always ready to answer back with a spirited reply. For seven long years he served his King faithfully, but then the war ended and the King no longer required his services.

"Here are seven ducats," said the King. "Go now and seek your fortune."

And the Princess, the King's only daughter, added with a laugh, "And when you find it, and have money, you will easily find a bride as well, and then you'll have everything you could ask for."

The little soldier was a merry and a brave fellow and he had a ready tongue, as I have said, but this time he could scarcely find words to utter. Seven ducats for seven years of faithful service hardly seemed enough to him.

"Very well, your majesty," he muttered to himself in the doorway, "but I shall be back and then you'll pay me the rest a hundred-fold."

And when he remembered how the princess had laughed, he was doubly bitter. "And you too, Princess," he said gruffly under his whiskers as he was going out the palace gate, "I'll talk it over with you one day and then we shall see."

And he turned around once more, as though he wanted to fix the royal castle and the way to it firmly in his mind, and then, with a smart stride, he set off to seek his fortune, an old cap on his head and his sword and a bag at his side.

The seven ducats did not last long, especially since the little soldier loved to sit in pubs and pay for anyone who sat down at his table. When the last ducat had been spent, he told himself that it was high time to begin looking for work. But where, and with whom? No one had work for a veteran soldier, and so he went from village to village until one day he wandered into a deep wood.

In the middle of the wood, in a clearing, stood a dilapidated old cottage. The little soldier was so hungry and thirsty and tired that he could scarcely walk, but he plucked up his courage, pounded on the door, and called out.

"Open up to a tired wanderer!"

The door opened and an ugly old crone stuck her head out. "What would you like, little soldier?" she said.

"What would I like, old woman?" answered the soldier. "Why a piece of bread and a little water so that I won't die of hunger and thirst, and a pile of straw in the attic so that I can rest for the night."

"You may have all of that and even more," said the old crone gruffly, "but you must work for it."

"With pleasure, old woman," said the soldier. "And anyway, I am looking for work with honest people."

"Come in then," said the old crone. "I shall give you work. It won't be hard, but if you do it well, you'll have enough for the rest of your life."

And so little soldier went in, and the old woman gave him food and drink and then she made a bed up for him in the attic.

Early next morning she woke him. "Get up, soldier, you've slept enough," she said. "Now it's time for you to do something as well."

The soldier jumped out of bed. "I'm ready, old woman," he said. "Just tell me what you want done, and I'll do it."

The old woman took him to the well behind the cottage. "I want you to lower yourself down into this well and bring me something out of it," she said.

"And what might that be?" asked the soldier in surprise.

"I'll tell you," croaked the old woman. "When you get to the bottom of the well, you will see three chambers. The first one is full of silver, the second is full of gold, and the third is full of precious stone. You can take as much as you can carry, but in return I want you to look for my old lamp with the blue light. It fell down the well and I need it, for it is the only one I have."

"Very well, I shall get it for you," said the soldier pluckily, and he jumped into the bucket hanging over the well. "Just let me down nice and slowly and don't forget to pull me back up again."

"I won't forget, soldier," croaked the old woman, and she began to let him down into the well. It was very deep, and the bucket went down, down, down into the depths for half an hour before finally hitting the bottom. The soldier jumped out and stood frozen to the spot. From three sides there poured a light so strong and bright that he had to close his eyes. When he opened them a short while later, he saw before him a room full of silver and beside it a room full of gold and next to that a room full of precious stones. With his head spinning from it all, the little soldier ran from one room to another, stuffing silver, gold and precious stones into his pockets, his shirt, and his boots with both hands. Very soon, he had so much treasure that he could scarcely walk. He dragged himself to the bucket and tugged on the rope. "Hey, old woman, I'm ready," he shouted. "Pull me up!"

"What about my old lamp with the blue light," she croaked. "Have you got it?"

"I forgot all about it," admitted the soldier, "but I'll find it right away."

Once more he returned to the rooms, and sure enough, in one of them, on the wall, hung an old lamp which gave off a blue light. The little soldier took it, went back to the bucket, and pulled on the rope.

"Hey, old woman, I have your lamp, now pull me up!" he called.

The little soldier got into the bucket and the old crone began to turn the handle of the crank. But it was very difficult, as you might well imagine, for the soldier had his pockets full of silver, gold and precious stones.

"You're far too heavy for me, soldier," whined the old crone when he was half-way up. "Send my lamp up first."

The little soldier didn't like the sound of this at all. "And what will happen with me?" he asked.

"I'll pull you up afterwards," croaked the old hag.

But the little soldier hadn't been born yesterday. He was wiser than that! "Oh, no," he said. "You might very well decide to leave me down here. What do you need the old lamp for anyway?"

"That's my business," snapped the old woman. "Either you send it up, or I leave you here in the well."

The little soldier knew that he was in trouble, but he didn't give in. "I won't send it up," he shouted back.

"Very well then," shrieked the old crone. "Stay there!"

And with that, she let go of the crank and the bucket with the soldier inside flew back down to the very bottom of the well. When it hit the bottom, the soldier was shaken to the very marrow of his bones, but otherwise he was unharmed.

Yes, the little soldier had been in many a tight spot in the war and he always managed to find a way out. But now he had to admit that he was at his wit's end.

"I won't get out this hole alive," he said. "Even with my pockets full of gold and silver and precious stones, I'll die of hunger down here. But before I die, I'll at least have a last smoke."

And he pulled a pouch of tobacco and an old clay pipe out of his pocket. The pipe had gone with him all through the war, and it was still with him now. He packed it full of tobacco, clamped it tightly between his teeth, and then began to pat his pockets for matches. But his matches were gone.

"That's a fine thing," grumbled the soldier disappointedly. "I won't even be able to have a last pipe before I die."

And then he remembered the old crone's lamp. He picked it up, and when he pulled up the wick, he almost dropped it on the ground in sheer amazement. For out of the blue

lamp jumped a little blue man who bowed to him and said, "What is your command, my master?"

"My command?" the little soldier cried. "Why get me out of this well, and be quick about it!"

"So be it, master," said the little blue man. "Just tell me where you wish to be."

"If I have a choice," laughed the soldier, "then I'd like to be where I came from."

No sooner had he said this that he heard a rushing sound in his ears and when he looked around him, he saw that he was standing in front of the royal castle with the lamp in his hands. The little man was gone.

But just then the little soldier had no need of him. He had his pockets and his boots full of silver and gold and precious stones, and so he took a room at the nearest inn. The next day, he bought himself a decent suit of clothing, a hat and a pair of boots. When he got dressed, pulled on his boots and set the wide-brimmed hat on his head, no one would ever have known that he was a veteran soldier who had served seven years for seven ducats.

"Money I have," said the little soldier proudly. "Now all I need is a bride."

And when he remembered how the King's daughter had laughed at him, he decided that he would try his luck with her.

"But first," he said to himself, "I will see if she is a good housekeeper."

The same evening, when the whole inn was asleep, the little soldier set the blue lamp on the table in front of him. As soon as he pulled on the wick, the little blue man jumped out of the lamp and said, "What is your command, my master?"

"My command?" laughed the little soldier.

"Bring me the princess, the daughter of our royal majesty, so that she can give my boots a decent polish."

"So be it, master," said the little blue man, and was gone. But before the soldier could turn around, he was back with the princess on his shoulders. The poor Princess was still asleep, and the little soldier almost felt sorry for her. But then he remembered how she had laughed at him, and he commanded, "Princess, I want my boots polished. For seven years I had to polish them myself and if they didn't fairly sparkle, there was great trouble! Now you try it."

And try it she did. She took the boots, she took a brush and the whole night long, she polished the soldier's high boots. It wasn't until the cock began to crow in the yard that the little blue man took her back to the royal castle.

In the morning, the Princess awoke with every joint in her body aching and she ran in tears to her parents and told them of a terrible dream she had had of how she had polished some soldier's boots the whole night.

The King shook his head when he heard this strange dream. "Perhaps it was a dream, and perhaps not," he said.

That night, to be sure, he had a bag full of peas tied to the princess's waist. The bag had a hole in it, and if the princess, God forbid! should move from her bed, she would leave a trail of peas behind her. Then they could easily discover where she had been.

That evening, when everything in the inn had gone to sleep, the little soldier once more put his magic lamp on the table, pulled up the wick, and commanded the little blue man to bring him the princess again, for he needed her to brush his coat.

"So be it, master," said the little blue man, bowing, and before the little soldier could turn around, he was back with the princess. Her eyes were closed and she was asleep, but the little soldier took no pity on her.

"Princess," he said, "my coat needs brushing. For seven long years I had to brush it myself. Now you try it."

And try it she did. She brushed the soldier's coat until the cock crowed in the yard. Then the little blue man took her back to the royal castle. On the way back, he noticed that a trail of peas led from the castle to the inn. He immediately guessed what had happened and he scattered peas in all the other streets of the town as well.

Next morning the princess awoke and complained to her parents in tears that once again she had dreamed of the same soldier and that she had had to brush his coat all night.

The King shook his head and went to the princess's room to see for himself. And sure enough, a trail of peas led from the room, across the corridor, through the courtyard and right to the square in front of the castle. But there it was lost, for the square and all streets were scattered with peas, as though it had rained peas in the night.

"That was no dream," said the King.

"No, it was certainly not a dream," said the Queen, and she told the princess to wear her slippers in bed. "And if you are forced to work again in the night somewhere," she told her daughter, "leave one of your slippers there and we shall find it."

That evening, when the whole town was sleeping peacefully, the little soldier stood his magic lamp on the table for the third time and pulled on the wick. When the little blue man appeared, he commanded him to bring the princess to wash his shirt. Before the soldier had time to turn around, the little blue man was back with the princess on his shoulders. The poor thing was sound asleep, but the little soldier did not feel the least bit sorry for her.

"Princess," he said, "my shirt needs washing. For seven long years I had to wash it myself. Now you try it once."

And try it she did. She washed the soldier's shirt until morning, and it wasn't until the cock began to crow in the yard that the little blue man carried her back to the royal castle. But not even he nor the little soldier noticed that the princess had left one of her slippers behind his bed.

Next morning the princess awoke and with tears in her eyes, she told her parents that she had dreamed about the same soldier again and that she had to wash his shirt the whole night.

The King shook his head, and so did the Queen, but then she remembered what she advised the princess to do.

"And what about the slipper," she asked. "Did you leave it there?"

The princess nodded. "Yes, I did. I hid it under the bed."

"Good," said the Queen happily, and at once she sent the palace guard into the town with orders to search every house from the cellar to the attic.

"The Princess has lost one of her slippers," she said, "and there will be a pouch of ducats for whoever finds it."

A pouch of ducats is quite a sum of money, and so the guards searched carefully until at last they found the slipper. It was lying in the little soldier's room under his bed. Before he realized what was happening, before he could pull on the wick of the magic lamp, the guards dragged him off to prison and they returned the slipper to his majesty the King. The lamp remained in the corner of the little soldier's room.

The King gave the little soldier a very short trial. "He shall pay for his audacity with his life and tomorrow, he shall be hung in front of the castle as a warning."

While the carpenters were preparing the gallows in the square, the little soldier was sitting in prison. He was sorry that he couldn't even have a last smoke before his death. He had tobacco and his pipe, but no matches.

"It would be even better if I had my old lamp," he said, tapping on the bars of his cell. Some old soldiers were standing around outside the window, and one of them leaned over and said through the bars, "What is it, my friend. What would you like?"

"How would you like to make a ducat, brother?" asked the little soldier. "I'd like to have a smoke, but I don't have a light. Would you be good enough to bring me my old lamp? It's in my room in that inn over there. If you do, I'll give you a ducat."

The old soldier was not one to scorn a ducat, and before the little soldier knew it, he was back with the lamp with the blue light. The little soldier was overjoyed. "Thank you, brother!" he cried. "I'll never forget you. Be sure to come tomorrow, and you'll see something you've never seen in your life before!"

The old soldier was somewhat surprised, for he had seen many a man hanged in his life, but even so he came the next day, and he wasn't sorry he had! When they took the little soldier to the gallows next morning, he cried out in a dauntless voice, "For seven long years, your majesty, I served you faithfully, and now you are sending me to my death. If that is your will, so be it. But grant me one last wish. Let me smoke a last pipe before I die."

The King was humiliated and nodded, "Very well, soldier, if that is your wish, then you may have a last smoke."

At this, the little soldier calmly took his tobacco and pipe from one pocket, and his old lamp with the blue light from the other, filled his pipe, clamped it firmly between his teeth, and then pulled at the lamp wick, so that he could light his pipe. No sooner had he done this than the little blue man jumped out of the lamp and said, "What is your command, my master?"

"My command?" laughed the little soldier. "Drive away the guards and give what for to all those ungrateful people, even though it be the King himself!"

And the little blue man started to work. All at once a huge club appeared in his hand and he began swinging it left and right with such abandon that everyone fled in terror. And fastest of all ran the King himself, but the club was always at his heels and it pounded and beat him until at last the King cried out for mercy. "Enough, soldier, enough! Stop that club, or it will be the death of me. I'll give you whatever you wish, gold, silver, precious stones, even my daughter as your wife."

The little soldier let himself be persuaded. "Enough, Blue Man," he commanded. "Now I have everything I could wish for, a fortune and a pretty bride."

The little blue man stopped beating and disappeared together with his club. The King sighed a great sigh of relief and then gave orders for a wedding to be prepared. It was a grand wedding, as royal weddings should be, and when it was over, the King gave his new son-in-law half his kingdom as well. And so, for his seven years of faithful service, the little soldier got more than seven ducats after all. He lived with his princess happily ever after and he always looked after his old lamp with the blue light as if it were a part of himself. And why not, when it had helped him to find all that fortune and happiness?

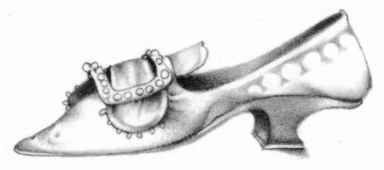

A LITTLE SOLDIER MARCHED ABOUT THE BEAR-SKIN RUG arm in arm with a princess. Both of them were glowing with happiness. When they came up to Willie, they both bowed and began to dance. The little soldier's sword and the princess's coronet sparkled so brightly that Willie had to rub his eyes. When he took his fists away, everything was gone and only the little girl was sitting on the bear-skin rug, asking for another fairy-tale. But Willie didn't want to read any more. So he said, "But you know, it's your turn now."

And so the little girl placed her finger to her lips so that he would be quiet and at that, something began to sing in the chimney. And then the still, quiet voice of the Wind began to tell a story. And this is what she told.

ONE-TOOTH, TWO-TEETH, AND THE SULTAN'S SON

Once upon a time, there were two old ladies who were so poor that they owned nothing more in the world than their little house beside the Mosque. When they were young and pretty, they were too poor to get married, and now that they were old, a wedding was quite out of the question. Both had white hair, wrinkled faces, and even their teeth had begun to fall out. The older sister had only one left, and so they called her Old One-tooth, and the younger sister had two left, and so they called her Old Two-teeth.

Old One-tooth had long ago given up all thoughts of ever getting married, but the younger sister, Two-teeth, was still trying to think of ways to find a husband. One day she had an idea. It happened to be a Friday, the day when all Muslims go to the Mosque to pray, and she said to her sister, "Listen, One-tooth, when the son of our Sultan goes by the house today on his way to the Mosque, I will pour water from the washbasin on his head, and then you must begin to shout, 'What have you done, my beautiful sister? You've poured the water you washed your face in right on the son of our Sultan. Now they'll have our heads for it!'"

One-tooth always did what her sister said without question, and so she replied, "Very well, little sister, I shall do as you wish."

And Two-teeth began to make ready. She poured clean water into a washbasin, then she added her best perfume and waited until the young Sultan's son rode by. As soon as he appeared, she quickly poured the water on him and One-tooth began to cry out, "O woe, beautiful sister! You have poured the water in which you washed your face right on the son of our Sultan! Now he will have both our heads for it!"

The Sultan's son heard of this perfectly well, but he was not angry. The water smelled so sweetly that he said, "How beautiful that face must be, if the water in which it was washed is so fragrant!"

And instead of going to the Mosque, he hurried quickly home to his mother. "Mother dear," he said, "I beg you, go to the little house beside the Mosque and ask for the beautiful maiden who lives there. I want her for my wife."

"But my son," protested his mother, "Only old One-tooth and her sister live there. But if you insist, I'll go there to see for myself."

And so the Sultan's wife went to the little house beside the Mosque. She was greeted at the door by One-tooth.

"Where is the maiden who poured water on my son yesterday?" the Sultan's wife asked sharply. "I want to see her."

But One-tooth was not frightened. "She is here, gracious lady, but no one may see her until she is married."

"Then show me her little finger, at least", said the Sultan's wife.

"That is possible," said One-tooth, bowing, and she opened the door to the next room a crack and said, "Beautiful sister, show the Sultan's wife your little finger."

And Two-teeth stuck a small white candle on which she had put several rings through the partly opened door. The candle looked just like the slender finger of a beautiful young maiden. The Sultan's wife was satisfied, said goodbye to One-tooth and hurried back to the palace.

"My dear son," she said, "you have chosen well, for your bride-to-be is a rare beauty. We shall prepare the wedding at once."

And so in the palace and in the little house beside the Mosque, preparations were made for the wedding. The very next day the Sultan's servants came to One-tooth with a sedan-chair. The bride, in nine veils, got into it and the servants carried her back to the chambers of the Sultan's son. There she was warmly welcomed by everyone and then they left her alone with the groom.

The young Sultan could hardly wait to see his beautiful new bride and so he flung aside one veil after another until at last he came to the ninth. When he lifted it, he cried out in surprise, for instead of a beautiful young maiden, he saw before him a wrinkled old woman with only two teeth.

"Who are you?" cried the Sultan's son.

"Your bride!" answered Two-teeth.

The young Sultan could hardly believe his eyes. He picked up Two-teeth and flung her out of the window as though she were a scare-crow. Poor Two-teeth turned several somersaults in the air and then landed head down, feet in the air right in the middle of a soft flower-bed.

As it often happens, one person's grief is another person's mirth. In the royal town, the Sultan was not the only ruler. There was also the King of the Flowers, Animals and Spirits. He had an underground palace near the Sultan's gardens and he ruled over his kingdom with his only son and his seven daughters. Yet everyone in his palace was very sad, for the King's son and heir to the throne had been ill for a very long time, and nothing could help him. He was suffering from a great, inexpressible sadness and nothing in the world of spirits or in any other world could make him laugh and shake off his melancholy.

But the good Prince was cured overnight, and the reason for his cure was poor Two-teeth. For just when the Sultan's son threw her out of the window, the son of the King of Spirits was wandering sadly through the Sultan's garden. When he saw her making somersaults in the air and then landing head down in the soft flower-bed, he burst out laughing for the first time in a long time. His illness suddenly disappeared, and the Prince returned gaily to the palace of the King of Spirits.

His sisters were amazed. "What happened to you, brother?" they asked. "Who has cured you of that evil illness?"

"That old woman who is lying in the Sultan's garden with her head in the flower-bed and her feet in the air," he laughed. And then he told his sisters what he had seen and why he had laughed so hard.

His sisters laughed too when they heard their brother's account, but because they were kind-hearted, they went to help the old lady on her feet again. The good Prince went with them.

"Since you've helped the old lady on her feet," he said, "you should also reward her for helping me to get rid of my melancholy."

"Gladly," replied the sisters, "but tell us, what should we give her?"

"Each of you give her a little of your own youth and beauty," said the Prince.

And the sisters did as their brother advised. One of them gave old Two-teeth beautiful hair, the second beautiful eyes, the third beautiful teeth, and when the last one had given her beautiful new clothes, Old Two-teeth was a lovely woman such as the world has seldom seen or will see. And then the daughters of the King of Spirits returned to their underground palace with their brother and good Two-teeth remained sitting on the soft flower-bed in all her beauty.

Just then the young Sultan awoke and went to the window to see what had become of his bride. But as soon as he looked out into the flower garden, he cried out in amazement. For amidst all the flowers sat a young maiden so beautiful that he could hardly take his eyes off her. He ran out to her to see if it wasn't just an illusion. But it was true, his bride was as beautiful as the day. The young Sultan took her to his chambers, asking her all the while, "Is it really you, my bride? How can it be that you are so different now?"

"Yes, it is I," replied Two-teeth. "You simply didn't look closely enough yesterday." And she smiled with a smile that made her look twice as beautiful.

And so the young Sultan received the most beautiful woman in the town as his wife after all.

And what about One-tooth, you ask? She came next day to see her sister in the palace, and when she saw her, she stood fixed to the spot. "Tell me, Two-teeth, how did you become so beatiful?"

What could Two-teeth say? She couldn't tell her sister the truth, because she wouldn't believe it anyway, and so she said, "When I saw how young my groom was, I went into a miller, gave him a piece of gold, and asked him to grind me into a younger woman."

Poor One-tooth believed her and without delay she ran to the miller and asked him to grind her too. But when she saw how the mill-stones ground everything to a fine powder, she was frightened. "Rather than that, I will remain One-tooth for the rest of my life", she said to herself.

And so One-tooth remained One-tooth and lived happily and contentendly as she had done before until she died. And Two-teeth lived happily and contentendly ever after, all the more so because she had got married after all, just as she had always wanted to. At least, that is how the story is told in this old tale of One-tooth, Two-teeth, and the Sultan's son.

IT WAS SATURDAY AFTERNOON and Mother and Father still hadn't come.

"They won't come till tomorrow," said Granny.

And so Willie had one more evening before the fire. But he almost missed it. Towards evening they had a visitor, one of Granny's friends, and she stayed for supper. After supper Granny and Willie walked to the main road with her. The sky was like black velvet full of twinkling little holes, which were stars. But Willie didn't pay much attention. He was afraid that he would get back too late to meet the little girl and he walked so quickly that Granny began to complain.

"You're going too fast for these old legs," she said. "What's the hurry?"

"I want to go to bed," replied Willie.

"If I could only believe you!" Granny muttered.

But when they got home, she put him straight to bed and then put the lamp beside him. "This is if you want to read," she said.

Willie blushed. "Thank you, Granny," he said and then he ran to the door to give her another good-night kiss.

When she was gone, however, he turned the lamp out again. The light from the fire was enough. He sat down on the bearskin rug, leafing through the book, and when he raised his head again, the little girl was sitting on the bear's head.

"There are a lot of stars out tonight," she said.

Willie nodded. "I noticed that too. There are more here than there are in the city. Were you ever there?"

But the little girl did not reply. She took a piece of paper Willie used for a book-mark and twisted it into a beautiful red rose. "Here", she said, handing it to Willie. "It's a present for you to remember me by."

Willie took the rose and to his surprise it didn't change to ashes in his hand, but remained a rose. He didn't know what to say, so he put the rose in the book and began to read very slowly and quietly. And this is what he read.

CINDERELLA AND THE GLASS SLIPPER

Once upon a time there was a merchant who was so rich that not even he himself knew how much money he had. He had a beautiful house in the middle of a beautiful garden. He had vineyards and fields, he had huge warehouses and full granaries. In short, he had everything he could think of, but his greatest treasure of all was his beloved wife and his one beautiful daughter, whose name was Ella.

But dear Ella was not just beautiful; she had more than just a pretty face. She also had a kind heart and so everyone was very fond of her. But her mother and father loved her most of all. Then there was her old godmother. Other people were somewhat afraid of the godmother; they said she was a witch, but to Ella, she was a good old fairy and whenever she wasn't at home with her mother and father, you could find her at her fairy godmother's little cottage.

And so Ella lived happily and contentedly and the days flew by in joy and delight. But one day, her mother suddenly fell ill. No one knew what the matter with her was, and even the best doctors in the land could not help her; not even the fairy godmother herself knew what to do. Before the week was out, Ella's mother closed her eyes forever.

Ella could have cried until her heart would break, but her unhappiness was just beginning. When her mother was sick and knew that she would never get well, she made her husband promise that he would find a new mother for Ella as soon as he could. The rich merchant promised that he would, and it wasn't long before he kept his promise. Within a year and a day he married a rich widow from the neighbourhood and Ella had a new mother and two new sisters.

Her new sisters were older than Ella and they weren't a bit pretty, but they put on grand airs as though they were princesses. Even their names were grand. The first was called Adriana and the second Belinda. The servants had to address them respectfully as "the Misses", but behind their backs they called them something quite different. They called the older one Spiteful Adriana and the younger one Vain Belinda.

At first, Ella let no one say a bad word about her stepsisters and she would apologize to others and to herself for their behaviour, but before a month had gone by, she preferred to say nothing, and before half a year had gone by, she went about the house with her eyes red from crying. And whenever she had a free moment, she ran to her beloved fairy godmother with her sorrows.

And with good reason! First her stepmother and her two stepsisters took away all her books, because they said she was always reading instead of working, and they sent her into the kitchen to sweep out the cinders. Next they took away all her clothes, because they said it was a pity to wear them in the kitchen, and so all she had left was a ragged old skirt. And finally they drove her out of her room, because they said that a pile of straw was quite enough for a kitchen wench, and so she had to sleep on the straw underneath the stairs. But the worst humiliation of all was that they stopped calling her Ella, and everyone in the house began to call her Cinderella. And the name stuck.

"It's nothing, girl," said her fairy godmother to cheer her up. "If you can bear it for a little while, everything will take a turn for the better, you'll see."

And she was right. For while the three sisters, spiteful Adriana, vain Belinda and beautiful Cinderella were growing up, in the neighbouring town the son of the old King was growing up too.

He was as sturdy as an oak tree, kind, courageous and gallant, just as a prince should be. Everyone loved him, and everyone called him Prince Charming.

Prince Charming was growing into manhood and it would not be long before he would ascend the throne in place of his father. The old King and Queen felt that their son ought to get married, and the Prince agreed. But where was he to find a bride?

"We shall hold a ball," the Queen decided, "and we shall invite all the eligible young maidens in the kingdom. Then it will be a simple matter to choose one of them."

The very same day the royal messengers were sent out to invite all the beautiful young maidens in the kingdom to the royal ball and a great wave of excitement and anticipation swept the land. But the greastet excitement of all took place in the household of the wealthy merchant. Drapers, silk-merchants, dressmakers, tailors, shoemakers, gold and silversmiths were constantly coming and going and the poor merchant had spent a good quarter of his fortune before he paid for everything that Adriana and Belinda bought. But for poor Cinderella there was hardly a groat left for a new duster.

After seven days of feverish preparations, both the sisters were more or less satisfied and they began to dress for the ball. Dear Cinderella helped them get ready. And when they were finally dressed and admiring themselves in the mirror, Cinderella couldn't help letting a sigh escape from her lips.

"Don't tell me you want to go to the ball too?" laughed Adriana.

Cinderella lowered her head and tears filled her eyes.

"Then we'll arrange an invitation for you!" cried Belinda sarcastically. "When the mice and the cats have a ball, then you shall too. But in the meantime, run to the kitchen and bring in the wood and take out the cinders!"

And she gave Cinderella a sound thump on the back to make her hurry.

Then both sisters got into the coach which was waiting for them and off they drove. Poor Cinderella rushed weeping to her fairy godmother.

"Now then, what's the matter?" said her fairy godmother, though she knew very well what had happened. "Don't tell me you really want to go to that ball?"

"Oh I do, I do," said Cinderella. "Just for a while."

"Then you shall," said the fairy godmother. "Run and bring me a walnut from the pantry."

"What could that be for?" Cinderella wondered, but she did what she was told and brought her fairy godmother a big walnut. The fairy godmother lay it just outside the door and then touched it with her cane. And Cinderella was even more astonished when the walnut suddenly turned into a magnificent golden coach!

"And now bring me the mouse trap from the cupboard," said her fairy godmother.

As if in a dream, Cinderella did what she was told. She brought the mousetrap from the cupboard, and there were six live mice running around in it. The godmother opened the door to the cage, and as soon as a little mouse ran out, she touched it with her cane and it changed into a beautiful horse. In the twinkling of an eye, six fiery steeds were harnessed to the coach. All that was missing now was a coachman to drive them off.

"Run to the kitchen and call the tomcat," said the fairy godmother.

Cinderella ran and called the tomcat. As soon as her fairy godmother touched him with her cane, he turned into a handsome coachman with long whiskers and glowing green eyes. He jumped into the driver's seat as if to say that it was high time they were going. But Cinderella was still standing in her tattered old dress.

"I can't go to the ball in these rags," she said bitterly.

"And why not?" said her fairy godmother, and she touched Cinderella's old dress with her cane. And in a flash, it changed into a splendid gown all of silver, as though woven of moonlight. On her head she had a diadem in the shape of a moon, on her finger she had a ring with a moonstone in it, and on her feet she wore slippers of glass.

"And now off you go and have a wonderful time," said the fairy godmother. "But one thing I must warn you of. Be home by midnight, or there will be trouble."

"I will, godmother," cried Cinderella happily, and with that, the coach drove off and disappeared into the darkness.

Meanwhile in the royal palace, the ball was already well under way. The music was playing, cavaliers danced with young maidens, but the young prince sat glumly beside his mother and father the King and Queen and refused to dance. The old Queen was already quite annoyed and she was just about to scold him when the doors at the other end of the ball-room opened and in stepped an unknown maiden in a magnificent silver gown which looked as though it had been woven of moonbeams.

The young maiden was so beautiful that all the dancers stopped, and even the musicians, as if on command, ceased playing, and before the guests recovered their senses, a good quarter of an hour had gone by.

But as soon as good Prince Charming saw the unknown beauty, he ran to welcome her. He bowed deeply before her, as though she were a queen, offered her his arm, and when the music started up again, they began to dance. And he danced with her the whole evening, and the whole evening he tried to find out where the beautiful maiden in the gown of moonbeams came from. But he found out very little, because whenever the Prince would ask, Cinderella replied that she was from Thumpton.

About eleven o'clock, the guests sat down to a banquet. Prince Charming didn't even touch his food, for he could only look at Cinderella, but Cinderella, who had had nothing like this for such a long time, ate heartily, and she would have eaten more had not the clock on the castle tower suddenly begun to strike half-past eleven.

Dear Cinderella was startled. She remembered what her fairy godmother had told her and she stood up from the table, bowed deeply to the Prince and all the guests, and rushed out. In her haste, she stepped on someone's foot and bumped into someone else. Before the Prince knew it, his lovely dancing partner was on the staircase and soon the jingling of her golden coach could be heard. By the time the Prince reached the staircase himself, there was not a trace of her anywhere.

"Where could that Thumpton be?" wondered the Prince when he returned to the palace. He had a map of the kingdom brought to him, but nowhere could he find Thumpton. With a heavy heart, he left the ballroom and the dance was over.

Meanwhile Cinderella arrived home without a mishap. Her fairy godmother was waiting for her, and when she touched the coach, the horses, the coachman and Cinderella's gown with her cane, everything was like before. The coach became a walnut, the horses became six little mice in a trap, the coachman became a tomcat, and the magnificent gown became just a dress of rags and tatters once more. Almost before Cinderella had time to tidy up the kitchen, the jingling of a coach was heard in the yard. Her sisters had returned from the ball.

"What a beautiful ball!" shrieked Adriana.

"And a princess came, even more beautiful than we!" cried Belinda.

"Just imagine, she stepped on my foot!" boasted Adriana.

"And she bumped into me!" said Belinda even more proudly.

"In a week, the Prince is holding another ball. It will be splendid!" said Adriana.

"And now undress us, and don't just stand there like a block of wood!" commanded Belinda, and once more, poor Cinderella had to start to work.

The week went by quickly in a fever of excitement and anticipation. The wealthy merchant had to spend a second quarter of his fortune before the two sisters were more or less satisfied. But poor Cinderella was left out again this time too. Her only reward

190

for helping her sisters get ready for the ball was even more tongue-lashing and more blows.

When they were finally dressed and admiring themselves in the mirror, Cinderella could not help letting a sigh escape her lips.

"Surely you don't want to go to the ball too?" laughed Adriana.

Cinderella only hung her head and said nothing.

"Very well, then, when the cooks and the scullery maids have a ball, you shall go too," said Belinda scornfully. "But in the meantime, run and fetch the wood for the kitchen and take out the cinders."

And with a sound smack, they drove Cinderella out of the room.

Soon both the sisters were sitting in their coach and on their way to the ball. Cinderella ran in tears to her fairy godmother.

"Now, now, what's the matter?" said the fairy godmother, even though she knew very well what the matter was. "Don't tell me you want to go to the ball again?"

"I do, Godmother," admitted Cinderella, "at least just for a little while, to talk with the Prince."

"Very well, then, you shall," she said. "Run and bring me a walnut from the pantry."

And so Cinderella went to the ball a second time. Everything was as it had been the week before, the coach, the horses, the coachman, but Cinderella herself was more beautiful than ever. This time she had a gown that seemed to have been made of pure sunlight, and on her head she wore a diadem in the shape of the sun, and on her finger she had a ring with a sunstone in it, and on her feet, slippers of glass.

"And now off you go and have a wonderful time," said the fairy godmother when Cinderella got into the coach. "But remember one thing. You must be back by midnight or there will be trouble."

"I will, Godmother," she promised, and in the wink of an eye she was at the palace.

This time too the ball was in full swing. The music played, the dancers whirled about the floor, and good Prince Charming was waiting on tenterhooks to see whether his beautiful dancing partner would appear or not.

And she did. Just when he was about to go outside to see if she was coming, the doors opened and into the ballroom stepped Cinderella in her gown of sunlight. The prince and his guests were even more astonished than the week before, and it was a good half an hour before they recovered their senses. From then on Prince Charming never left her side. He danced with her the whole evening, talked with her the whole evening, and the whole evening he tried to discover what her name was and where she was from. He found out very little this time too, for the beauty in the gown of sunlight always replied that she was from Smackston.

About eleven o'clock, the guests sat down to a great banquet and this time too, Prince Charming only sat and gazed at Cinderella, while she ate and ate with great gusto. And she would have eaten even more had the clock on the tower not suddenly struck a quarter to twelve.

Cinderella was startled. She remembered what her fairy godmother had warned her, and with as few words as possible, she said farewell to the Prince, bowed, and ran off. In her haste, she stepped on someone's feet and almost knocked down someone else. Prince Charming ran after her, but when he reached the staircase all he saw was Cinderella's golden coach disappearing down the avenue of trees.

"I wonder where this Smackston is?" said the Prince when he returned to the ballroom. He had a map of the kingdom brought to him, but he looked for Smackston in vain. Sadly, he left the room and the ball was over.

Meanwhile Cinderella had arrived home and she jumped out of the coach just at the stroke of midnight. Her fairy godmother was waiting for her and she touched the coach, the horses and the coachman, and Cinderella's gown with her cane, and once more Cinderella was standing in her rags. Then she ran to the kitchen to tidy up.

Before she could turn around twice, she heard the jangling of a coach in the yard. Her sisters had returned from the ball, and they went straight into the kitchen.

"What a beautiful ball!" cried Adriana. "Even more beautiful than the first."

"That Princess came again, and she was even more lovely than before," shrieked Belinda.

"And when she left, she stepped on both my feet," boasted Adriana.

"And she almost knocked me down," said Belinda even more proudly.

"And in three days the Prince is giving another ball," said Adriana. "It will be the most splendid yet."

"And now get us ready for bed quickly, and don't just stand there like a lump of cheese," shouted Belinda, and poor Cinderella had to start working again.

The three days went by in even greater excitement and agitation than before. It cost the wealthy merchant so much money that another quarter of his fortune was gone, and even then it wasn't enough for the older sisters. But poor Cinderella didn't receive so much as a new hairpin. There was only more work for her and besides that she had to suffer constant scolding and blows from her stepsisters as she helped them get ready.

When at last they were prepared and admiring themselves in the mirror for the last time, Cinderella remembered Prince Charming and sighed.

"Don't tell me you want to go to the ball too?" laughed Adriana.

Cinderella hung her head and blushed.

"Go on, admit it, and we'll send you to a ball when the rag-and-bone men have one!" said Belinda scornfully. "But in the meantime, run and fetch the wood and take out the cinders."

And with a slap they drove Cinderella out of the door. And right afterwards, the coach clattered out of the yard and the sisters were gone. Cinderella was left alone, and after a while, she ran off as usual to her fairy godmother.

"Now then, what's the matter this time?" asked her fairy godmother. "You don't mean you want to go to the ball again?"

"I do, Godmother," admitted Cinderella. "I'd like to have at least one dance with Prince Charming."

"And so you shall," said the fairy godmother. "Run to the pantry and bring me a walnut."

And so for the third time, Cinderella went to the royal ball. Again she had a magnificent coach of gold, horses, a coachman and a new gown which was even more beautiful than the ones before. It was as though it had been woven of the very stars themselves, and on her head she had a diadem of tiny stars and a ring of starstone on her finger. And she had the glass slippers on her feet, as before.

"Off you go, now, and have a wonderful time dancing," said the fairy godmother as the coach was leaving with Cinderella. "But don't forget, be home by midnight or there will be trouble."

"I will," promised Cinderella, and almost before the words were out of her mouth, she was at the royal palace.

As usual, the ball was already well under way. The music was playing, the dancers were whirling gaily about the floor, and good Prince Charming was standing by the door watching for his beautiful partner to appear.

As soon as he saw her coach drive up, he rushed to open the door for her, and then led her ceremonially into the ballroom. Cinderella entered in the gown of stars and the astonishment and amazement of the guests and musicians was even greater than three days ago. Before they could recover their senses, a good hour had gone by.

Once more Prince Charming danced the whole evening with the unknown beauty. The whole evening he talked with her and tried to discover where she was from and what her name was. But he was unsuccessful, for to every question the beautiful maiden in the starry gown replied that she was from Slapston.

About eleven o'clock, the guests sat down to a richly laid table and as usual, Prince Charming merely sat and gazed while Cinderella ate and ate. And she would have eaten even more had she not suddenly heard the clock on the palace tower begin to strike midnight.

Cinderella was most alarmed. She jumped up from the table without a word and rushed to the door without bowing to anyone. In her haste, she knocked down two of the guests, and then she disappeared down the stairs.

This time, however, the Prince was quicker than before, and he rushed out to the staircase right behind her. But when he arrived there was not a trace of his beautiful dancing partner.

All he could find was her glass slipper which she had lost while rushing out of the palace. And in the distance, he could see a flash of white, as though someone were running away.

It was Cinderella. On the last stroke of twelve the fairy godmother's magic power ended and the coach, the horses and the coachman were suddenly gone and in their place remained only a walnut shell, and a cat and some mice which scurried away in all directions. And Cinderella's gown of stars disappeared too, leaving her once more in her tattered old rags. Only one glass slipper remained on her foot. Cinderella hid it under her apron and ran home barefoot.

At home her fairy godmother was waiting for her with a frown on her face.

"Just a moment more and there would have been trouble," she said sternly.

Cinderella felt very sorry. "Don't be angry, godmother," she said, "but I was having such a wonderful time at the royal palace that I didn't notice what time it was."

"I believe you," said her godmother. "But run along to the kitchen now. Your stepsisters will soon be back from the ball."

While Cinderella was running home, Prince Charming stood on the steps of the royal palace with the glass slipper in his hand. "Who could that beautiful maiden who danced with me be?" he asked himself.

And he ran to look for Slapston on the map. But he found nothing by that name, so he left the ballroom with a heavy heart. The dance was over.

All the guests went home. Almost before Cinderella could look around her, a coach pulled up into the yard: it was her step-sisters coming home from the ball. For the third time they came into the kitchen to look for Cinderella.

"That was a simply marvellous ball!" cried Adriana.

"And that beautiful Princess came again, for the third time!" said Belinda.

"Imagine! She knocked me down when she ran out at midnight!" boasted Adriana.

"And me as well!" said Belinda even more proudly.

"And she lost a glass slipper on the palace staircase," said Adriana.

"And tomorrow Prince Charming is going to go through all the land to find the one the slipper fits," said Belinda.

"If only it would fit me!" sighed Adriana.

"Or me!" sighed Belinda.

"Or me!" said Cinderella very quietly.

"What did you say, you Cinderella!" both her step-sisters shouted at once, and they drove her under the staircase with blows.

The sisters were telling the truth, for the very next day Prince Charming set out with a huge retinue to look for his unknown partner. He went from town to town, from village to village, from castle to castle, and everywhere he tried the glass slipper on all the young girls. I can't tell you how many he tried it on, but there must have been a lot of them, for he rode around his kingdom for a whole year.

And exactly a year and a day after the last ball, the Prince's suite stopped at the house where Cinderella lived with her step-sisters. Their father graciously welcomed the Prince and then the ceremonial trying on of the slipper began.

The first one to try on the glass slipper was Adriana. She tried as hard as she could to squeeze her foot into it, but all her efforts were in vain. The slipper would not go on. She threw it down angrily, but, wonder of wonders, the slipper, though it was made of glass, did not break. Cinderella, who was standing shyly in one corner, picked it up and gave it to her second step-sister.

Belinda tried even harder than Adriana, but she fared no better. Try as she might, the slipper would not go on. Finally she flung it angrily on the floor, but the slipper, as before, did not break. Cinderella, who was standing shyly in the corner, picked it up and asked softly, "Whose turn is it now?"

"You try it!" cried Adriana angrily.

"Yes, perhaps it will fit you!" shouted Belinda scornfully.

Poor Cinderella didn't know what to do, but Prince Charming told her to sit down and try the slipper too. "I want every maiden in the house to try it on," he said kindly.

And Cinderella did as she was told. She put the glass slipper on the floor, slid her foot into it, and the slipper fitted like a glove. Everyone was amazed, and Prince Charming was most amazed of all. He could scarcely believe his eyes, but his disbelief did not last for long, because from under her apron Cinderella pulled a second glass slipper just like the first one and slipped it onto her other foot. That one too fitted like a glove.

No sooner had she put on both slippers than the magic of her fairy godmother began to work again and her tattered rags changed immediately into the magnificent gown which looked as though it were made of the stars themselves.

And at last, spiteful Adriana and proud Belinda recognized who the beautiful Princess at the ball was, and it was a wonder that they didn't burst from sheer shame, anger and envy. But Prince Charming was joy and happiness itself. He knelt before Cinderella as before a Queen and asked for her hand in marriage.

"With pleasure, Prince Charming," said Cinderella, blushing with delight, and she gave him her hand.

And what happened after that you can imagine for yourself. The very same day Prince Charming took his long-sought bride back to the royal castle and along with her he took her good fairy godmother, who had done the most to bring about their happiness.

And within three days there was a royal wedding. It lasted seven days and seven nights, but their happiness lasted for the rest of their lives. And even today, this story is told about it.

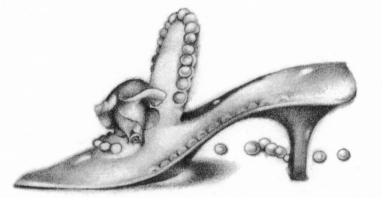

THE LITTLE GIRL'S ROSE SMELLED SO SWEET

that it made Willie sleepy. With half-closed eyes he saw that she had on a gown made of the stars themselves and glass slippers on her feet.

"So you are Cinderella," he whispered.

The little girl laughed and it sounded like little bells ringing. "You were only dreaming, but why do you ask so many questions? Just listen."

And she put her finger to her lips as a sign for him to be quiet and listen. From the chimney came the still, quiet voice he knew so well, and the Wind began to tell a story. This is what she told.

THE WOODCUTTER
AND THE DRAGONS' PRINCESS

Once upon a time there was a poor widow who had an only child, a son. His father had been a woodcutter, and the son became one too. As soon as he was able to hold an axe in his hands, he went with the other villagers into the mountains to cut wood, and every day he worked very hard to earn a plate of food for himself and his mother.

The years went by and the lad grew into a handsome, stalwart young man. But even though he was old enough to marry, he had no wife. For who would give their daughter to such a poor man? Even so, he did marry, and better than many a prince. Listen! This is how it happened.

One day, early in the morning, the young woodcutter set out for work as usual. He put on his straw sandals, put a hat upon his head against the sun, threw an axe across his shoulder and set off with the others into the mountains. It was a beautiful, clear day, but as the woodcutters drew near to the foot of the mountains a fog suddenly descended on them. The fog was so thick that they could hardly see a single step in front of themselves. The woodcutters walked and walked and walked through the fog, but soon they became hopelessly lost. Without even knowing how, they suddenly found themselves in a strange place and before them towered a high, steep cliff with an opening that looked like a huge gate.

The woodcutters were afraid to go any further. "What if this is the Dragons' Gate that old men talk about?" they whispered to themselves in dread, and rather than go on, they turned about and hurried back the way they had come.

199

But the son of the poor widow was not afraid. "Since I'm already here," he said to himself, "I shall have a look," and he went through the opening in the rock.

As soon as he was on the other side, the fog lifted and a bright world full of light opened up before him. The sound of distant music, as if someone were gently beating a gong or playing a flute came to him on the breeze. The young woodcutter followed the sound of the music until all at once he saw, deep in the valley before him, three green lakes full of clear, sparkling water flowing into each other over dancing waterfalls.

The lad stopped by an old pine tree and gazed at the beautiful scene. All at once the waters in the middle lake became agitated and then a huge turtle came to the surface. It looked around carefully, and then sank once more into the depths. A short time afterwards a huge green dragon appeared on the surface. It too looked carefully around and then disappeared once more.

And very soon afterwards, the waters of the lake opened for a third time and a very beautiful young maiden came to the surface. She climbed onto a lily pad and there she sat, combing her long, dark hair.

When the young woodcutter saw this rare beauty, he could no longer contain himself and he sighed out loud. But before his sigh had died away, a bolt of red lightning flashed across the lake and the beautiful maiden disappeared.

The woodcutter was very unhappy. All at once he felt that he could not live without the beautiful maiden. He ran to the lake, closed his eyes, and leaped in head first.

When he opened his eyes, he found himself on the bottom of the lake. But there was no water anywhere, and everything was just as bright and clear as in the world above. And in the distance, the woodcutter saw a huge, high palace. When he reached its gates, however, he saw a sight which filled his heart with terror. For in front of the palace lay two black dragons.

As soon as the young woodcutter appeared, one of the dragons disappeared into the palace. A short while later it reappeared and led the woodcutter inside. He found himself in a magnificent hall full of gold, silver, turquoise, rubies and diamonds. And in the middle of the hall, on a throne, sat an old green dragon.

"Who are you, my good man? Speak, how did you get here?" asked the old dragon.

"I am a poor woodcutter, honoured sir," answered the widow's son. "I lost my way in the fog and came to the three green lakes and in one of them I saw a beautiful maiden, and when she disappeared under the water, I jumped in after her."

"That beautiful maiden is the Dragons' Princess," said the green dragon, "and because the Princess has sworn to marry the first man who sees her face, you are in luck, for you may have her if you want her."

How could the young woodcutter not want such a beautiful maiden, when he had dared to jump into the water after her? So he nodded happily and a wedding was prepared immediately.

And so the son of the poor widow married the Dragons' Princess.

After the wedding, the young woodcutter lived for a long time with his beautiful wife in joy and contentment. Only one thing made him sad, and that was that his old mother could not share his happiness with him. One day he could bear it no longer, and so he said to his beautiful wife, "Today my mother has her eightieth birthday. Please let me go and visit her for at least one day. Then I shall return to you right away."

And the Princess replied, "Go, and make her happy. And take this little vase with you. When you need something, just ask and the little vase will give it to you."

The woodcutter's old mother had already wept away all her tears for her son. She thought that he had perished somewhere in the mountains, or that wild beasts had eaten him. And so her surprise and joy was all the more when, on the very day of her birthday, the door opened and her son stood on the threshold.

It wasn't long before the whole village had come running to welcome him back. Many questions were asked, but the young woodcutter mentioned not a word about what had happened to him.

"I have come to celebrate my mother's birthday," he replied to everyone. "And you are all invited too!"

And then, in secret, he took his magic vase and whispered something into it. In the wink of an eye, the table was spread with jugs full of good wine and plates with four and twenty courses of the finest food. And while they were eating and drinking the best company of actors entertained the guests with six and thirty different acts. It was something the like of which the village had never seen before.

But while the guests were eating and drinking and the actors performing, the young woodcutter and his mother disappeared without leaving a trace behind them. For the woodcutter had whispered again into his magic vase, and in a flash they were both on the shore of the dragons' lake. Then they jumped in together.

And from that time on, all three of them have lived happily and contentedly until today, for in the kingdom of dragons, no one ever dies.

NEXT MORNING WILLIE FOUND THE ROSE pressed between the pages of his book. It still smelled as sweet as the night before. But his evenings before the fireplace were over. At noon, his Mother and Father came for him. Willie tried to persuade them to let him stay longer, because he didn't want to go back to the town yet. But his Mother said, "But Willie, you're all better now."

And his Father was rather sharp with him. "As it is, young fellow, you've had an extra fortnight's Christmas holidays. Now you must go back to school."

Even Granny joined in. "That's true, and anyway, he ran around the house all day and didn't stay in bed. Not even in the evening. Every night I found him sleeping on the bear-skin rug by the fireplace. But he deserves credit for one thing. All of a sudden he's become a marvellous reader. He read for whole evenings at a time. And nice and loudly and clearly."

When Granny said this, she laughed as though she knew everything. But she knew nothing, she couldn't know anything. Willie never told her who he was talking with those evenings. What if the little girl wanted to come back sometime? Perhaps in the summer holidays, when he would come to Granny's cottage in the woods once more. Or next Christmas, when he would again sit on the bear-skin rug by the fireplace reading the books which he would get under the Christmas tree.

And so Willie returned to the town with a great secret and even greater expectations. For a whole year long he looked forward to his Granny, to her cottage in the woods, but most of all to the crackling fire, its fiery little men and the little girl with hair like gold and eyes like deep green pools.

Did he ever see her again, you ask? I don't know. Willie has never told me, and for the time being he is keeping it to himself. But who knows, perhaps one day he will tell me, just as he told everything I have told you in this book.

Good night!